ONWARD AND UPWARD

It is 1953, and the Cobridge family is ever-growing. Paula and William have settled in their flat, and Nellie and James's daughter Bella is becoming a rebellious youngster. As her teacher, Paula believes she is suffering from dyslexia. She also thinks the child is somewhat neglected by her overly busy parents. William is engaged in his coronation ware at the ceramics factory and all seems to be moving onward — until disaster suddenly hits the family. How will Nellie survive alone?

CHRISSIE LOVEDAY

◆

ONWARD
AND
UPWARD

Complete and Unabridged

LINFORD
Leicester

First published in Great Britain in 2014

First Linford Edition
published 2015

A catalogue record for this book is available
from the British Library.

ISBN 978–1–4448–2371–4

Published by
F. A. Thorpe (Publishing)
Anstey, Leicestershire

Set by Words & Graphics Ltd.
Anstey, Leicestershire
Printed and bound in Great Britain by
T. J. International Ltd., Padstow, Cornwall

This book is printed on acid-free paper

1

1953

It was a Sunday in early February. At Cobridge House, the family were sitting down to lunch.

'So, what sort of a week did you have, Paula dear?' asked Nellie, matriarch of the family.

'Not bad actually. The new school is one hundred percent better than the old place.'

'I think it stinks,' announced Bella, the seven-year-old daughter of Nellie and James.

'Really Bella,' her father remonstrated. 'That is no sort of language for the lunch table. In fact, it's no sort of language for you to use at all.'

The child looked angry.

'What am I supposed to say then?'

'Nothing at all, unless it's something

1

good.' James was quite strict in the way he'd treated his children, though at twenty-four, William was way past being controlled by his father. Bella, a rather late arrival in the family, was certainly still being controlled by her fifty-one-year-old father.

'I think Paula needs to have a word with you about Bella's progress in school. Not now though,' said William. The little girl was in Paula's class at the local primary school.

'No, not now. Perhaps you can spare a few minutes this afternoon?' Paula didn't want to speak in front of the child.

'What are you going to say about me?' Bella demanded.

'I'll talk to your mother.'

'I absolutely deserve to know what you plan to say,' the little girl told them all. She rose from her seat and stamped her foot. They ignored her and continued to eat.

'Lovely beef today,' William said, trying to bring things back to normal.

'Certainly is,' Paula agreed.

The meal continued with general conversation about the factory and everyone's plans for the coming week. The child, having been ignored, sat down again and continued to eat. When she had finished she said, 'Can I get down now?'

'Please may I leave the table' is what you should say. Really Nellie, this one has no manners at all.' James was annoyed with his daughter.

'Well can I, or not?'

'Ask properly and then you can go.'

'Please may I leave the table?' Bella repeated dutifully.

'Yes, dear. You can go now. I'll get some coffee organised if you'd all like to go through to the drawing room.' Nellie was trying hard to keep the peace.

It was a lovely room. Recently redecorated in pale blue and with a patterned carpet picking out the blue and peachy colours, it was very restful. There was a huge china cabinet stretching along one wall containing the family collection of Cobridge china. There was one of every item the factory had made over the years and it was now bursting at the seams.

'It looks as if you'll need a new cabinet soon,' remarked Paula. She was a relatively recent addition to the family, having married William the previous summer. She was still getting used to living in part of the huge house in their apartment upstairs.

'Either that or we stop bringing the pieces home,' James said with a smile.

'It's the coronation collection that's made the difference. Till then, the cabinet coped very well.' William was proud of his work that was to contribute to the factory's future.

'And we're not even there yet. Another few months to go. I hope we're going to cope with the orders that we expect.'

The two men began to talk about the future and how the factory was going to bring in extra work. Paula drifted away from them, waiting for Nellie to come back with coffee. Naturally she was interested in the factory and had loved the tours she'd been given, but it was really rather remote from her. She was relieved that William had left her to get on with her career in teaching and was enjoying life at her new school.

'Coffee's on its way,' Nellie said as she came back. 'Sorry for the delay. Cook is arguing with Sarah about something and nothing. She'll bring it in soon. Now, what did you want to say about Bella?'

'She's not doing as well as we might have hoped at school. She is rather naughty and her work isn't up to standard at all. I suppose me being related to her isn't much help. She often calls me 'Paula' in class. I don't like that. It's almost as if she expects special treatment because of it.'

'I'll have a talk with her. Why do you think she's behind the others?'

'Partly because she seems unable to concentrate. I'd actually like to have her tested for dyslexia. I think she's having difficulties with words. I've seen a few signs of it in her written work.'

'Oh dear me. Isn't that known as word blindness? Is there anything we can do about it?'

'If she is dyslexic, then yes. There are a number of aids we can use.'

'Really? Then we must get her tested. Whatever it costs, let us know. Can you arrange it?'

'I'll look into it. I hope that's her only problem. Her behaviour is certainly something that also needs attention. I suppose I can deal with it, eventually.'

'I'll certainly have a word or two with her. Thank you for telling me all of this. I'm not sure when I can do much to help. It's really busy at the factory at the moment. I'm rather tied up by work.'

Wisely, Paula didn't respond to her words. She privately thought that Nellie spent too much time worrying about the factory and not enough time with her daughter. Bella was such a pretty little thing, and twisted everyone's arm to let her do exactly what she wanted. Spoilt wasn't in it. Paula had recognised it immediately but had been pleased to see that James corrected her at the table. Still, at least she had the go-ahead to call for help in getting Bella tested for dyslexia.

A sulky-looking Sarah came in with the coffee tray and dumped it down on a table. She left it there and stormed out of the room.

'Well, really,' Nellie complained.

'I'll pour it, shall I?' offered Paula, wanting to prevent further upset.

'Thank you, dear. I can see the girl's in a bad mood but there's no call for that sort of behaviour.'

'No worries. I'm happy to pour out some coffee. You like yours with milk, don't you?'

'Yes please. And I'll have some sugar today. I need it with all this temper that's flying round. Someone else I have to have words with.'

She handed the coffee cups to the

two men and took milk and sugar over to them. She frowned at William when he put two spoons of sugar into his cup. He grinned at her and she smiled back, knowing she would speak to him later.

Cobridge House had been built by William's grandfather, after whom their son had been named. It had been built before the end of the previous century, at great expense. It was a massive building with servants' quarters as well as guest rooms and several large reception rooms. In those days, a whole team of people were employed to clean and cook for the family, most of whom lived in. There was a cook, a house-keeper, several maids and someone who came in to clean on a daily basis.

Nellie had been one of those maids, a time she would never forget. She had benefited from the attention paid to her by James, her husband of many years. It had been a difficult time when she had arrived at the house as his wife, becoming the lady of the house and managing the servants. Now in her late forties, she was very much in charge and expected the remaining two staff to do their duty without complaining. After all, she had given them a decent home and there were only the three of them to be looked after now. There was also a woman who came in to clean each morning, and her daughter-in-law Jenny sometimes came to look after Bella. She had been nursemaid to William when he was a baby, so she was well used to the work.

All in all, it seemed to work well and Nellie spent a lot of time at the factory, overseeing the decorating and designing new items to add to the range of fine bone china manufactured there. Their reputation was very good in the Potteries and their china had maintained its high price. James was the managing director of the company and seemed to find things to do with himself, tucked away in his office. William was also making his own mark, having undertaken their new range of coronation specials.

'How are you getting on with

producing the special plates?' she asked her son. Sundays seemed to be the only time she had to ask him about his work.

'Fine. As you know, we're using some of the approved badges they've produced as lithographs. Plus some special gilding on the edges of the plates. I think they'll look really classy and should go well. There are some mugs too. The same lithograph and gilded handles.'

Paula sat sipping her coffee and listened to the *factory talk*, as she thought of it. She had tried to be interested in what they were saying but it left her somewhat cold. She longed to get back into their apartment and do her school work, but she knew that wouldn't please William. So there she stayed, getting up only to top up their coffee cups. She gave thought to the problem with Bella. The child was totally spoiled and behaved accordingly. Perhaps it was just that she had a problem with reading and writing, but it didn't entirely help with her behaviour.

'What do you think, Paula?' Nellie asked.

'Sorry?' She jumped. Her mind was miles away.

'I asked if you wanted to stay for tea?'

'Would you think me very rude if I said no? I have some school work to finish for tomorrow and I really need to get on with it.'

'You're much too conscientious, darling,' William said affectionately. 'It would do you good to take a break.'

'Why don't you stay and I'll go up and do my work?' Paula suggested. 'I can always come down again when I've finished, if you want to stay that long.'

'If you really want to. If that's all right with you, Mother?'

'Of course it is, dear. You go up. I'll go and tell cook the plan.'

'Thank you. I do hope you don't mind. I'm sure you can find things to talk about that don't involve me.' She rose and left the family in the drawing room and escaped up to their apartment.

It had been made using three of the

guest rooms, and a kitchen and bathroom were added. It was a simple design and she had chosen light colours to make the most of the daylight. She loved it and had put in lots of bright cushions which were piled up on the sofa. Following the trend towards having one large room, their dining table was at one end of the lounge and the sitting area was at the other end. It was all very much smaller and far less grand than the rooms downstairs but at least they had their own front door, which could be closed against un-welcome visitors. Paula sighed and got out her school books. She was in no hurry to go downstairs again and rather hoped that her husband would come to join her before too long.

* * *

'What do you make of this nonsense about Bella?' Nellie asked her husband. 'I've never noticed her bad behaviour, have you?'

'She's got no manners,' James announced. 'As we saw at luncheon. You're always too busy to train her.'

'I beg your pardon? Train her? She isn't some sort of dog. I never had these problems with William.'

'Think on it, dear. William was never any good at school. In fact, he was something of a problem to all concerned. That is, until he went to America. After that, he seemed a bit more sensible.'

'Well, he met Paula soon after that, didn't he? She's usually such a sensible girl.'

'Don't mind me, please. Carry on talking about me as if I'm not here. I suspect I was quite revolting as a child. Possibly as a young man too.'

'You're quite right, son. I despaired of ever having you to work in the factory, but you came through, whatever was bothering you. You never did tell us about what happened.'

'Something I want to forget about. Let's just say I had a bad time and lost all the money you'd given to me. It certainly taught me a long-lasting lesson. Now if you don't mind, I think I'll go and see how Paula is getting on.' He rose and went upstairs. Nellie and James stared at each other.

'Did you know about that?' asked James.

'No. I had no idea. I just thought he'd spent all his money on frivolous things. Well, whatever happened, he came back a better person. But none of this helps with Bella. What do you think we should do?'

'Up to you, dear. I don't get involved with the child's behaviour. I think I'll go to my study now. Look over some papers.'

'Oh dear. I'd better tell Cook everyone's deserted me. Never mind. I'll sort out something.'

Nellie sat looking at the fire. She took it for granted that it would always be lit ready for them and tea would be brought when she rang the bell. Remembering the days when she worked down below stairs, she knew there would be little rest for the two women working in the kitchen. The washing-up would take them a lot of time, though at least now there was plenty of hot water. She remembered the days when all the water had to be boiled on the stove. Even that had now changed. There was a modern gas cooker she'd had installed with six burners on the top and two ovens. It was considered to be top-of-the-range and designed to make life easier for the cook. Hence, they only kept one cook and one maid these days. Several of the main rooms were shut off, as they were no longer used, which also meant the one cleaner who came in daily could cope easily. How times were changing.

Feeling relaxed for the first time since . . . well she couldn't remember when, Nellie thought about her family. Joe, the elder of her brothers, was settled on his farm with his wife Daisy. Their daughter Sally seemed well-adjusted and went to the local village school.

Then there were Ben and his Jenny. He had returned from the war badly affected, but now he was healthy and fully recovered and worked as a studio potter, turning out wonderful things in the factory every day. Jenny was always brilliant with little ones and often came to look after Bella. Her own pair of children were also growing up fast, one at school and the other a lively toddler. Lizzie, her sister, had surprised Nellie somewhat by having a son. She'd often said she didn't want children, but then, people changed so often when they were married. Her marriage to Daniel was a huge success. He had been badly injured in that damned war too. She smiled to herself as she thought of scatty Lizzie being a nurse and looking after him.

'Oh Mum,' she said softly. 'You'd have loved to see all the family settled down like this.' She felt tears burning at the back of her eyes and wiped them away quickly. It would never do to let anyone see her crying, especially not the servants. Just as she was thinking of them, there was a knock at the door. Sarah came in.

'You ready for tea yet?' the girl almost snapped.

'It's just me now. You might take Mr James some up to his study as well. Sarah, what's wrong? You don't seem to be yourself today.'

'Nothing, Missus Nellie. I'm all right.' She paused. 'It's Cook, missus. She's gone round the bend.'

'What on earth do you mean?'

'She's gone all stroppy and she's moaning all the time.'

'I'd better come down and see what her problem is. Oh dear, I hope she isn't thinking of leaving us.'

'Good riddance is what I'd say.'

'Sarah, please. You wouldn't like to have to do all the cooking as well as serve at table now, would you?'

'Couldn't do it.'

'Very well, I'll come down with you now and see Cook.' She rose from her seat and followed the maid to the kitchen. The cook was sitting at the kitchen table holding her head in her hands. As Nellie entered, she lifted her head and tried to stand up.

'I'm sorry, ma'am,' she said.

'What's wrong with you? Do you actually feel ill or something?'

'It's nothing. I'm sorry. Just feeling a bit down, I suppose.'

'It's more than that. I can tell.' Sarah was hanging round in the background, her ears tuned to hear all that was going on. 'Go and make some fresh tea Sarah,' Nellie instructed. 'Now come into the sitting room and tell me what's wrong.' Somewhat shakily, Cook followed her into the little sitting room, once used exclusively by the housekeeper. 'Sit down and tell me what's wrong.'

'I'm just finding everything a bit much to cope with. There's only me to do everything and I'm finding it all too much.' The middle-aged woman began to cry. Nellie, quite used to dealing with such matters, told her to stop crying and to talk to her. 'Sorry, ma'am. I think I need an 'oliday.'

'Perhaps you do. But this is hardly the time of year to go anywhere. It's horrible weather and I certainly wouldn't recommend you go away just now. You have two weeks off in the summer in any case.'

'It's a long time till summer,' she said sadly.

'Do you want more help in the kitchen? Suppose we employ a new girl to help you?'

'That'd be a help. That Sarah, well, she argues summat chronic whenever I ask her to do owt she doesn't think she should do.'

'Like what?'

'I asked her to make your coffee after lunch for starters. You should have heard the abuse I got.'

'I think I did hear some of it. I'll have a word with her. And I'll look into organising a new helper for you, if that's what you'd like.' Sarah came in with a mug of tea for the cook. She put

19

it down on the table rather unceremoniously. She looked at the two women and waited for one of them to say something. 'Thank you, Sarah,' Nellie said graciously.

' 'sorright. So what's up with her?'

'I'll speak to you later. Go and sort out the tea things for the rest of us.' Sarah went out looking like thunder.

'See what I 'as to put up with?'

'Do you know what's wrong with the girl?'

'I think she's gorn soppy over one of the tradesmen what calls here. He came yesterday and she missed him. Gave me a right mouthful for not calling her to see 'im.'

Nellie sat thoughtfully for a moment. 'You drink your tea. I'll have a word with Sarah and see what's to be done about her.'

'Thanks, Missus Nellie. I'm sorry to bother you with my worries.' Nellie smiled at her and got up, leaving her still sitting. She gave Sarah a good talking-to and said she would have to leave if she didn't improve her way of going about things. With a sigh, she went back to the drawing room and sat down heavily.

'I must be getting old,' she said to nobody. 'Forty-six and I feel like ninety.'

2

Exasperated, Paula took a deep breath and spoke again to Bella. 'You are very naughty, Bella. You must apologise to Janey right now.'

'I don't see why. She started it. She was making fun of me.'

'But you must never hit anyone, whatever they may have said to you. Do you understand?'

'Shan't. Shan't 'pologise.' She stamped her foot and folded her arms as if that was the end of it.

'Then you must go out of my classroom. Go and stand in the corridor outside. I'll speak to you later.' The child remained exactly where she was and with the same sullen expression on her face. 'Go on, Bella. Outside now. I don't want you in my room.'

'I'll tell my mother of you. Tell her what a rotten, mean person you are.'

'You don't frighten me, child. Tell her what you like. Now, go outside. Immediately.' The child sulkily went to pick up her bag and looked as if she was going to do as she had been told. 'You can leave your bag. Go and stand outside the door.'

'I hate you, Paula. I really hate you.' She left the room and stood outside, sticking her tongue out at Paula's back. Some of the children saw her and sniggered.

'Anyone looking at Bella will be punished as well. Now please, get on with your work. Do you all know what you're supposed to be doing?' Nods came from the children and soon peace was restored. Paula gave a small sigh. She must get someone to see Bella. It really wasn't working, having the child in her class. It felt like an abuse of her professionalism, but she knew something must be done. From the corner of her eye she could see Bella was doing her best to get the attention of the other children. She rose and stood against the glass panel of the door, looking at the rest of the class.

'All right, two more minutes and we'll see what you've all done. Are you all right now, Janey?'

'Yes, thanks, miss. I wasn't teasing Bella, honestly.'

'I know you weren't. Shall we start with you? Would you like to read out what you've written?'

The class went on until it was almost lunchtime. Paula went to the door and told Bella she was allowed into the room again. Barely subdued, she came back in and the other children ignored her. She danced to her place and started fooling about again.

'Bella, you've been warned about your behaviour. Settle down now, until it's time to go for lunch.' She began to say something and then thought better of it and shut her mouth again. The rest of the day went reasonably well and with no more events.

She talked to William about his sister that evening. 'She is getting unbearably

24

rude and keeps on answering back. I really don't know what to do with her.'

'Talk to Mother. If you can find her, that is. She's working late tonight so I don't know who's supposed to be looking after the child.'

'She's probably in the kitchen with Cook. That seems to be the usual system. What happened to you when you were little?'

'I think Jenny lived in then. She would have looked after me. Ben was living with Nellie's Mum at the time, ages before they got together.'

'Things have really changed, haven't they? Your parents used to have loads of staff. Seems strange to think of. My Aunt Wyn was your housekeeper and she was never replaced, was she?'

'Nope. I suspect people don't want live-in jobs any more. I heard Mother talking about getting another maid to help Cook. She's finding things difficult at the moment.'

'Really? I can't see why. There's only your parents and Bella.'

'Don't ask me. I know nothing about hiring servants. Have you got work to do this evening or shall we watch television?'

'I'll just do the washing up and we can watch something.'

'I'll dry, so it'll be finished more quickly.'

They continued to chat over the dishes. Paula knew she was lucky that he was willing to help. He could have been more like his father, who never did anything at all to help in the house. Nellie had offered them the chance to have her cleaner to come into their apartment but Paula had preferred to do it all herself. She had said it made her feel more married. William didn't care at all and left her to organise the place as she liked.

'So, should I say something to Nellie? About Bella?'

'How would you deal with any other child?'

'Well, if it was one occasion, I'd have told her off and dealt with it within the school. If it happened a second time, I'd have written to the parents and probably called them in.'

'And how many times had Bella been like this?'

'I've lost count.'

'Then yes, tell Mother. You can't go on like that.'

'I feel it seems like a personal failure on my part though. For goodness sake, she's only a child.'

'The trouble is, she's also a relative. That's what makes the difference. And you say she has a problem?'

'Yes, that's true. I have told the appropriate person about it and she is coming to test Bella as soon as possible. That's for dyslexia, of course. But that doesn't solve my problems with her.'

'Come on. Let's see what the television has to offer. I think *I Love Lucy* is on. You like that, don't you?'

'Yes I do. I know it's rather silly, but so what? And thanks for listening. I'll try and talk to your mother tomorrow.'

Nellie was working late again the next day so Paula had to wait again. Bella was marginally better behaved that day so the sense of desperation she had been feeling had dissipated somewhat. She prepared their supper and left it all ready to heat when William arrived home. He, too, was rather late and she switched on the television, waiting for the transmission to begin. Very soon she fell asleep and when her husband arrived home, she was lying on their couch with the television playing music to the test card.

'Hallo, you,' he said, leaning over her and kissing her cheek.

'Oh, goodness. I'm sorry. I'll get supper right away.'

'You must have been exhausted. Not like you to sleep like that. An early night for you, my girl.'

'Only if you come and keep me company,' she told him with a smile. 'Supper won't be long. Just needs warming. You go and change and I'll pour you a drink. Busy day?'

'Fairly. The first large batch of plates ... the coronation ones came out today. They look terrific. Should sell well. Oh sorry, I should have brought one home to show you. Mind you, we'll need to get a move on if we're to make good sales.'

'I didn't see your mother again today. She was working late.'

'Oh, you mean about Bella? You'll catch her sometime, no doubt.'

'No doubt. Hopefully before she reaches secondary school.' Paula felt a little despairing of ever sorting out the child while her mother was working so hard. At least she assumed Nellie was working hard, but she did not understand how the endless meetings could possibly be called working. To her, talking was something you did during lunch breaks and working happened in the classroom. But then, she was just a school teacher and had little concept of industry. She watched as the vegetables came to the boil, realising her role in life was much less glamorous than that of Nellie Cobridge. She speculated about the future. Would they have children of their own? How would she manage then? She'd hate being stuck at home on her own all day. Maybe having children was something they needed to consider carefully. William came and stood behind her. He slipped his arms round her waist and nuzzled her neck. She turned round and kissed him.

'I think an early night would be in order,' he said softly. 'What do you think?'

'Sounds like a plan. But first, we have a meal to eat. I must drain the vegetables. Go away now.'

Paula dragged out the colander and tipped the pan into it. Soon they were both sitting eating and enjoying the savoury stew.

'This is good. Did your mum teach you to cook? I seem to remember coming to your rescue with a roast once and that doesn't seem so long ago.'

'I had a crash course before we were married. I can't say I'm much of a cook now, but I am getting better. And that time you came to my rescue . . . it was when Mum went into hospital. It was the beginning of everything, really, wasn't it?'

They reminisced about their courtship and how things had turned out. Her mother had cancer and her aunt, the one-time housekeeper at Cobridge House, had given up working and gone to live with her sister. It seemed all was well now and the two sisters seemed very happy together.

'It was good of your aunt to go and live with your mother,' said William. 'It meant you could come here and we could be married. All good. Is there a dessert?'

'There's some fruit or cheese. I haven't made a pudding, I'm afraid.'

'Oh,' he replied, somewhat disappointed. 'I'll get some cheese.'

'I'll get it. Sorry.' She rose from the table and cleared the plates. Paula knew

William was used to having a full meal each evening and still felt a little put upon that she was expected to produce a pudding as well as a main course, and all this after working full-time at school. It certainly couldn't last if she was to continue to work and she wasn't about to give up her job. She produced some cheese and biscuits and delivered it to him.

'Aren't you having any?' he asked.

'I don't want to end up putting on weight, so no. I ate a perfectly good main course.'

'I suppose you think I'm greedy, don't you?'

'Well, no. I suppose it's a case of what you're used to really.'

'I'll try to moderate what I eat in future. I don't want to get as large as my father.'

'He has certainly put on a good deal of weight. Looking at that picture taken when he was about your age, you'd hardly recognise him as the same person.'

'Really? I hadn't noticed particularly. Mother stays ever the same. She's aged a bit of course, but she's still small and wiry.'

'She's quite elegant though. Always looks nice too. I suppose she makes me feel a bit inadequate really.'

'Rubbish. You're absolutely fine. Maybe you need to go shopping a little more often.'

'Oh yes? And when am I supposed to fit that in? By the time I get home from school, it's time to start making some sort of meal for you. At the weekend, I have to clean through and there's always schoolwork to fit in between everything else.'

'Then we should get some help. Get a cleaner or something.'

'But my mother always managed on her own. When Dad was killed during the war, she had a job as well as looking after me.'

'Times have changed though. I'll have a word with Mother about getting someone to give the place a clean through. I'm sure one of the people she has could spare time to come up and give it going-over.'

'But I don't want anyone else coming in. It seems like a sort of invasion of privacy.'

'It's a case of you not being used to having someone. I've always had people in and out of my space. People to cook meals. Cleaners and someone to do the washing and ironing. It's quite normal to me.'

'I suppose so. Mum did everything in our house.'

'Exactly. You never minded that, did you?'

'It was different. I lived in Mum's house, and naturally she did things for me. You and I are married and it's now my job.'

'You're being silly. We need some help if you are going to continue to work. The alternative is for you to give up work and stay at home.'

'No. After all the training I did? Don't be silly. Besides, I love my work.'

'Then you must have someone to help. I insist.'

'I'll give it some thought. Now, if you've finished, I'll clear the table and do the washing-up.'

An hour later, William had put on the television and was slumped in front of it. He hadn't come to help Paula clear up and she felt annoyed. She had banged about in the kitchen and put things away noisily, all to no avail. He was sitting down and refusing to acknowledge her activities. She realised he was making some sort of point. She slipped onto the couch beside him and waited for him to show her the affection he had shown her before they'd eaten . . . before they'd had their argument about having help.

'I might go down and see my father,' he announced. 'I need to speak to him about the production of various coronation stuff.' He rose and left her sitting in front of the television. Paula sighed and got up to get her school stuff. If she was to be left alone, she may as well get some work done. She looked at the pile of books in her bag and took them out.

It was almost ten o'clock before William came back. He smelt of whisky and she knew exactly what would have happened. The two of them would have sat in James's study, drinking the evening away and chatting about some sort of nonsense.

'I'm ready for bed,' he said, somewhat slurry in his speech. 'Are you coming?'

'I'll just finish this and I'll be with you.' Paula was not about to be bullied into anything.

She continued to finish marking her books and left him to go off to bed alone, then gave a sigh and put the books away. She hated it when she felt left out of things. She was such a small part of this family, with their factory and everything that went with it. They had no social life of their own. Her friends, such as they were, were all connected with school and didn't interest William at all. Somehow, she needed to up her game and find something more in common for the two of them.

Paula went to bed to find her

husband snoring gently. She settled down beside him and lay awake for some time, trying to think of ways that she could make things better. Maybe having some help might release her time a little. By the time she fell asleep, she had decided to go ahead with William's plans to speak to Nellie. After all, she had always had help and would never think any the less of Paula for doing the same thing.

By the following weekend, William was very involved with his coronation memorabilia. He was having meetings with various people and spoke of little else. He had been working late most evenings and Saturday was taken up with even more meetings. Paula decided to spend the day with her mother and aunt and set off to see them after breakfast. William had already left for work and so she set off without telling anyone. Why should she worry? was her last thought.

'How lovely to see you,' her mother greeted her happily. 'Is William not with you?'

'He's working. I've given myself the day off, too, so here I am. How are you?' she said as she followed her mother through to the sitting room.

'I'm fine. Wyn's gone into town to do some shopping. I'll put the kettle on to make some tea. Or would you prefer coffee?'

'Tea's fine. So how are you, Mum?' she repeated.

'I'm fine. All the better for seeing you. How are you getting on?' she asked.

'Bit fed up if I'm honest. Sorry, I shouldn't have said that.'

'Course you should. I want to know the truth. What's wrong?'

'Oh nothing serious. I s'pose I'm just still getting used to my new life. School's great except for Bella. You know, Nellie's youngest. She's a veritable pain in the you-know-where. Nellie's given me permission to get her tested for dyslexia but I'm afraid she may have other problems. She keeps calling me by my first name, which gets the other kids in the class all excited.'

'Can't you talk to her mother?'

'Finding her in is another matter. She's all so wrapped up in the wretched factory that she's never got time for her. She's happy enough to pay for treatment, but that's not what the child needs. Oh, kettle's boiling. Sorry, I shouldn't go on about things.'

'Paula, dear, if you can't talk to me it's a bit of a poor show.'

'Thanks, Mum. I miss having you there to talk to.'

'And I miss hearing about your days. I used to love our chats. But everything's all right with you and William?' Paula looked away. 'Paula? It is all right, isn't it?'

'Oh yes. Of course it is. I just feel like a bit of an appendage to the factory. It's Cobridge's first and I'm somewhere way down the line.'

'That's not too healthy. What else do you talk about?'

'I don't really know. I was thinking the other night, we need to find something we can share in. Maybe I should take more interest in the factory, but they do make me feel like an interloper.'

'Oh, Paula my dear. I'm so sorry. It sounds a bit grim.'

'Oh I'm all right really. Just having a fit of the blues I guess. He wants to get a cleaner too.'

'I hope he isn't complaining about the state of the place.'

'Not at all. It was me who was moaning. All because I hadn't made a pudding one night.'

'Oh my dear.' Her mother was laughing now. 'You are in a bad way. Do you want some recipes? I'll sort some out for you. Now drink your tea and let's talk about something else.'

'I'm sorry you see it as a big joke. I was being serious.'

'I know you were, love. If everything was all sweetness and light, I'd be much more concerned. Are you going to stay for lunch?'

'If you don't mind. Yes, please. I need a complete break from that place.'

'I'll do another potato. It's a stew, so we'll make it spread.'

'Lovely. Thanks, Mum. Now, tell me about what's been going here.'

* * *

William came home expecting to find Paula busy cooking lunch. He called out to her but the place was empty. He looked around and saw it hadn't been cleaned or tidied. He ran down the stairs and went into the kitchen. 'Anyone seen Paula?' he asked.

'No, Mr William,' said Cook. 'Haven't heard her around all day.'

'Is Mother in for lunch?'

'I don't think so. Said she was going shopping this morning and would get something in town. Your father is out too. You want me to find something for you to eat?'

'No, thanks. I'll be fine. I just wonder where my wife has gone to.'

'P'raps she's gorn shopping.'

'Maybe. Yes indeed, that'll be it. I

suggested she might go shopping earlier this week. Thanks, Cook.'

He went back upstairs and peered into the fridge. There were some eggs and cheese so he decided to make himself an omelette. Whistling to himself, he whipped up the eggs and grated some cheese. He quite enjoyed a little gentle cooking. He put it onto a tray and took it into the lounge and sat down on the sofa to eat it. He put the tray beside him and lay back. Within seconds he was fast asleep and lay there slumbering until Paula came back at four o'clock.

3

Nellie awoke on Sunday morning and sat up. James was still fast asleep and she rose as quietly as she could. She put on her dressing gown and went down to the kitchen to make some tea. She liked sitting enjoying an early cup of tea on her own, without the staff chatting to her. It was her time to relax and plan her day. Once Bella was up, the peace was usually shattered. She thought about Paula's comment the previous week. She hadn't spoken to her daughter-in-law since then and hoped the problems had sorted themselves out or at least that Paula had managed to sort them for her. She was a nice girl and William seemed very happy. At least that was one less worry to plague her. Her son seemed to be stepping up to the mark too. His interest in the factory had also pleased both her and James, and his work on the coronation things seemed to going very well.

'Oh, you're up already Missus Nellie,' Cook said as she came into the kitchen.

'I wanted some tea.'

'You should've rung the bell and one of us would have brought it to you.'

'I think I can just about remember how to make tea,' Nellie laughed. 'Come and sit down and have a cup yourself.'

The two women, of similar ages but with a very different status, sat companionably talking about trivia. Then Nellie asked her cook something that had been plaguing her.

'About Sarah. You were quite full of anger last weekend. Is she not behaving properly?'

'She's all right I s'pose. Can be a bit of pain. But to be honest, Missus Nellie, like I said, there's too much for just the two of us here.'

'Yes, well I did say I'd look at getting another girl to help you. I should have done something this week but life is rather busy at present.'

'Well, if you can. I must say, I'm not really at my best just now.'

'I'm sorry to hear that. What's wrong?'

'It's my feet. Some days it's all I can do to stay standing.'

'Perhaps we'd better get the doctor to look at them.'

'It's me bunions, you know. Terrible aches they give me.'

'Then I'll definitely look at getting another girl who can help you. And you must sit down a bit more. Use a stool or a chair when you can.'

'There's summat else.'

'Oh yes?'

'I don't really like to say about it.'

'Go on.'

'Well it's your little 'un. Miss Bella. She's becoming a bit of a problem.'

'Bella? What's wrong with her?'

'Well, she's always 'ere. Comes 'ere after school and seems to stay 'ere till it's nearly 'er bedtime. She isn't easy to look after. Not like Mister William used to be. Always into some mischief or other.'

'I see. Perhaps Paula can help us out here. I'll have a word with her. She teaches her, so perhaps she can take her up to the apartment when she comes home. Leave it with me. Now, I'd better go and dress and see if James is awake yet.'

Nellie went upstairs to their bed-room. James seemed to be fast asleep and she dressed without waking him. She glanced at the time as she put on her watch. Eight-thirty. She'd leave him till nine, then wake him. He needed his rest, she thought, smiling fondly at her husband. She went down to the break-fast room and looked at some magazines. They were specifically for manufactur-ers of china and often provided useful bits of information. She made notes of some of the ideas in there and then rang the bell for breakfast. Sarah arrived with a tray, which she put out on one side.

'Thank you, dear. Could you take some tea up for James please? It's time he was awake now.'

'Me, missus? You want me to take tea up for the master?'

'Oh leave it. I'll take it if there's a problem. Go on with you.' Nellie poured a cup and took it up to her husband. 'Come on, sleepyhead. Time you were up. James? Come on. Wake up.' But he didn't move. She put the cup and saucer down on the bedside table. 'James? James, wake up. Oh for pity's sake.' She touched him. He felt cold. Very cold. She gave a shudder. 'Oh no. James, you can't leave me. Not like this. We're much too busy at the factory and there's too much for me to do on my own.' She felt tears burning her eyes. She reached for the bell and rang it. Sarah came up and knocked at the door.

'Come in. It's the master. He's been taken ill. Please ring the doctor and tell him to come urgently. Right away. You understand?'

'Yes, missus. Right away.'

'And come back here when you've called him.'

The girl ran off down the stairs. Nellie didn't move but sat holding her husband's hand. She needed William here. Sarah could go and knock on their door when she came back. She kept muttering his name but in her heart, she knew what had happened. After what seemed an age, Sarah came back.

'Cook says is there anything you need?'

'No. Go and knock at William's door. Tell him to come here immediately.'

She turned and left the room and Nellie heard her run across the corridor to the door of the apartment. She heard her hammering at the door and eventually heard it being opened. Time seemed to stand still.

'Mister William. Can you come quick to Missus Nellie and Mister James's room? She says you're to come right away.' Sarah's voice sounded slightly strange to the listening Nellie.

'What's wrong?'

'I don't know. Please come over right away,' she begged.

Clad in his dressing gown, he followed her into his parents' room. 'What is it?' he asked.

'It's James. I can't wake him.' She was still sitting on the bed, holding his hand. 'I've got the doctor coming but I'm afraid it's too late.'

William crossed over to her and reached to feel his father's brow. It felt very cold.

'Let's see what the doctor says. Maybe he's had a stroke or something. Come on, Mother. Don't worry. He'll soon put us in the picture. I'm going to dress quickly and I'll come straight back. Will you be all right?'

'Yes. Yes, you go and dress.' Nellie was speaking very quietly and William touched her hand as he left.

He rushed over to his own room and flung some clothes on, telling Paula what was happening as he did so. She also got up and dressed so she could also go over to her in-laws. He went back as the doctor was arriving.

'Morning to you all. Is he in here?'

'Yes. Please ... go in.' William followed him and Paula stayed outside.

'Morning, Nellie. What seems to be the problem?'

'He's cold. I can't wake him.' She seemed to have lost her voice.

'If you go and stand by your son, I'll examine him.' He took out his stethoscope and listened. He moved it across to the other side of his body. 'I need an ambulance,' he told them. 'There's a very faint heartbeat and I need to get him to hospital. Where's the phone?'

'You mean he's still alive?' Nellie said, hardly daring to believe it. 'It's in the hall. The phone.'

'Right.' He left the room and ran down the stairs. They heard him calling the hospital and demanding an ambulance to be sent as quickly as possible. He murmured something about a heart condition and then hung up. He ran back up the stairs and searched in his bag for something which he took out and sprayed into James's mouth. It seemed to revive him slightly and Nellie held her breath.

'He isn't . . . well . . . dead then?'

'Not at the moment. But he is very ill. I'm just hoping we can do something for him at the hospital. The ambulance should be here very soon.'

Nellie twisted her hands together, showing that she was worried despite her calm face. William was standing near the door, looking anxious. He heard a noise and ran down the stairs to open the door. He noticed Cook and Sarah peering through the kitchen door, also looking worried.

'Come in,' he said to the ambulance men. 'Upstairs, and the door is opposite you.'

'Thank you, sir.'

The two men ran up the stairs carrying something rolled up. William assumed it was a stretcher. They'd be hard pressed to carry his father down on that, he thought. He was a rather large man, after all.

'Ah, good. We need to get Mr Cobridge to hospital as soon as possible.'

'Right you are, sir.'

'If you'd like to leave us to it, m'am,' said the doctor. 'We'll soon have him in the ambulance and I'll follow behind.'

'Can't we come too?' asked the very worried Nellie.

'I'd suggest you come later on. Give us a chance to check on him. You come when you like but you won't be able to do anything for some time. Why not have some breakfast? I expect you haven't eaten yet.'

'Er no, we haven't. All right, I'll leave you to it.' Nellie rose from James's side and left the ambulance crew to deal with things. She left the room, taking William's arm as she left. He looked at her in surprise. Her arms felt so thin, and suddenly she seemed to have shrunk.

'Hallo, Mummy. What's all the fuss?' Bella came out of her room, bouncing and shrieking somewhat. She ran up to her mother and began to pummel her. 'What's going on?' she demanded.

'Your father is unwell. He's going to hospital. The ambulance men are here to take him.'

'I want to go as well.'

'Well you can't,' William snapped. 'None of us can go.'

'I want to go!' yelled Bella. 'I want to go in an ambulance.' She turned to look at her mother. 'Please can I go, Mummy? I can keep Daddy company.'

Nellie looked at William despairingly.

'I'll see if Paula can look after the child,' he said. 'Come on, Bella. Let's see if Paula has got any breakfast.'

'I want ice cream. I'm not going if she hasn't got ice cream.'

'Not for breakfast. You'll have the same as everyone else. Toast and marmalade.'

'I won't eat that. I hate marmalade. It's horrible.'

William took hold of the girl's hand and led her into his apartment. He knew Paula wouldn't be best pleased, but it was an emergency. He called out to his wife and she came to see what the trouble was.

'I wondered if you could look after Bella for a while? My father has to go into hospital and Mother is obviously worried.'

'Of course. Come on through, Bella. Have you had any breakfast yet?'

'No. I want ice cream. Strawberry ice cream.' Paula looked at her.

'I haven't got any ice cream. Certainly not at breakfast time. I'll find some cereal for you, and then there's an egg. Would you like an egg?'

'No. I want ice cream.' She began to chant 'ice cream, ice cream' until Paula lost her temper.

'There isn't any ice cream and if you don't want cereal, then you'll go hungry. Now, go and sit down in the lounge.' She spoke firmly and to everyone's surprise, Bella did as she was told. 'Can you get her something to play with please?' she asked her husband. 'And some clothes. She can't stay like this all day.'

William went to Bella's room and picked up various items of clothing and some toys. He took them back to Paula, who instructed the child to get dressed.

He left them to it and went back to his father's room to see what was happening. His mother was packing a few items James might need. She got his shaving kit together and wondered if he would ever use it again. She wasn't kidding herself that he was going to be using it for a while, but it made her feel better.

'Have they taken him down now?' he asked.

'They're putting him into the ambulance. Oh William, what if he doesn't survive?'

'Don't think like that, Mother. I'm sure they'll do everything they can. Now, do you want to come to us for breakfast? Bella is being fed by Paula and you are welcome too.'

'I don't think so, dear. I couldn't eat anything. I'm going to go to the hospital soon. If you could keep Bella, that would be the most help you could be to me.'

'Sure. Let us know what happens, won't you?'

'Of course I will. I'll go down and tell Cook and Sarah the latest news and then I'll go to the hospital.'

He watched as his mother went down the stairs. He really ought to go with her, but that would mean leaving Paula with his little sister, and he knew that would not be a good idea. Knowing how Paula was feeling about the child at the moment, he didn't want to leave them alone together for too long. He went back into the apartment and saw Bella sitting quietly on their sofa. He raised his eyebrows to Paula. She shook her head, telling him to make no comment.

'Any breakfast going?' he asked.

'I thought we'd just have toast today if that's all right with you.'

'Oh, all right then. No bacon? It is Sunday after all.'

'I'll do you some if you really want it. I thought you may not . . . with the worry of your father and all.'

'No, you're right. It'd probably stick in my throat. Toast will do fine. What about you, Bella? Do you want some toast?'

'I've said. I want strawberry ice cream or nothing.'

'Nothing it is then,' replied William.

Paula put some bread under the grill and stood watching it. She had already put out butter and marmalade and some plates. William went and stood behind her, putting his arms round her middle as usual.

'Shall I make some coffee?' he offered.

'Yes, please. I did boil the kettle earlier but it's cold again now.'

The two of them worked together and Bella sat watching them, saying nothing. She still looked sulky and cross. They took their food to the table and left her sitting on the sofa. At last she got up and went to sit at the table.

'I want toast,' she demanded.

'Really?' said Paula. 'And where's the missing word?'

'Marmalade.'

'Bella,' William said in a cross voice.

'Speak properly and use your manners.'

She looked sulky again and got up and left the table. 'I'm going down to see Cook. She won't make me starve.' She flung open the door and let it slam behind her.

'Really. My father's right. She hasn't any manners at all. I'd have been smacked within an inch of my life if I'd behaved like that.'

'Nothing new from that young lady,' Paula replied. 'Perhaps you can see now how it feels at school.'

'I'm sorry, but I can't really say anything to Mother at the moment. I wonder how Father is?'

'Do you think he'll survive?'

'He looked pretty bad to me. Hardly any pulse at all. I thought he'd actually passed on when I saw him, but the doctor could hear his pulse. I think it's a case of fingers crossed. I'm sorry; it must remind you of when your mother was so ill.'

'Maybe. Have you had enough?'

'Yes, thanks. I'd like more coffee

though. Then I'd better go down and see what Bella's doing.'

In the kitchen, Cook was nearing the end of her tether. Bella was sitting at the table, her arms covered in flour and a liberal spreading of the white stuff around the floor and table.

'Keep it in the bowl, like I showed you.'

'It's fun,' said Bella, ignoring her words and showering flour over the table again.

'I'll have to start again. Making pastry is an art,' Cook grumbled. 'Not something for you to play with.'

'Whee!' the child screamed in great excitement as a new shower went all over herself. She was almost out of control when William arrived on the scene.

'What on earth are you doing?' he shouted at his sister.

'It's great fun. Watch me.' She dipped her hands into the bowl again and threw a handful over the kitchen floor.

'Stop it right now,' he ordered.

'Shan't. It's fun. You never want me to have fun.'

'Too darned right I don't. Get down immediately and wash your hands. Then you get a dustpan and brush and clear up some of the mess. I don't know what your mother would say.'

'Nothing. She doesn't care about me. She's too busy working. Making the money to keep us all.'

William listened to the child's words and realised she was probably right. Their mother was a self-imposed busy lady and spend far too much time at the factory.

'Go and wash yourself. Have you got a dustpan somewhere?'

'Sarah will get it out. Go on, girl. Get it out.' Sarah went to the cupboard and collected it. She gave it to William while he stood over his sister, supervising her hand-washing. She was not a happy little girl but she realised there was no getting out of her brother's orders. Meanwhile, Cook took the bowl of what was supposed to be pastry and tipped it into the waste bucket. She handed the bowl to Sarah, who took it to be washed. With very bad grace, Bella took the dustpan and brush and began to sweep up her mess. Her brother was a hard task master and wouldn't let her stop until it was clean. The child scowled and grumbled throughout the process but at last it was acceptable.

'Right. Now you'll come upstairs with me and behave yourself.'

'Thanks Mister William,' said Cook gratefully. 'I'll get on with cooking lunch now, though I'm not sure if anyone'll be here to want it.'

'Paula and I will be here, and Bella too. I'm not sure if Mother will be back, but you can put some aside for her, can't you?'

'Course I will.'

He left the kitchen, taking his little sister firmly by the hand. She went with him quietly, as if she knew she'd lost the battle.

4

Nellie sat in a waiting room at the hospital. She was alone and felt very worried about her husband. Their own doctor was with him as well the hospital staff. What on earth would she do if he didn't survive? He was responsible for the whole factory; but though she had no idea of what he did with his time, he was ultimately in charge. William, though he was working well, had none of his father's ability to run the whole place. Perhaps it would be down to her. But could she do it all alone? She very much doubted it. Would anyone take notice of her? She was only a woman, and everyone knew you needed a man to do man's work. At last a doctor came to see her.

'Your husband has had a severe stroke. We think he'll be all right, but he is drastically changed from his old self.

He might improve but at the moment, he is a very sick man. If you want to come through, you can see him now.'

Feeling very frightened by the man's words, Nellie followed him. There were screens all round her husband and various machines seemed to be making noises. James was lying there with his eyes closed, looking absolutely dreadful. Nellie caught her breath.

'Can he hear me?' she whispered.

'Probably. We're never too clear on that but we assume he can,' said her own doctor.

'Hallo, dear,' she said to him. 'How are you feeling? Better, I hope.' The words were a struggle to get out and she had little idea of what to say.

'Go on. Talk to him as if he were wide awake. The sound of your familiar voice might help him.'

'It's a good job it's a Sunday. We don't need to be at the factory today.'

'Good. Go on,' encouraged the doctor.

'William and Paula send their love,

and Bella too. They are all worried about you and want you home again.' She stopped there and rose. 'I'm sorry. I can't do this.' She ran out of the hospital room and stood by a window in the corridor. She couldn't bear to see her husband lying there like that. He looked so unwell and so unlike himself. The tears fell unchecked and she groped in her bag to find a hand-kerchief. She heard someone coming up to her and she wiped away her tears. She turned to the doctor and said, 'I'm sorry. I think I should go home now and leave him in your good care. He isn't listening to me anyway and I feel there are things I need to do at home.'

'Very well, Mrs Cobridge. We'll call you if there's any change.'

'Thank you. I think my son will come in later.' Now appearing cool and calm, Nellie walked away and went back to her car. She gave a sniff and started it, driving home again quite quickly. She told William the latest news and asked him to go and see his father later.

'Where's Bella?' she asked.

'She's in with Paula.'

'I need to explain to her what's wrong with her father. Send her down to me, will you?'

'Of course. It will be good if you spend some time with her. I think she may feel a bit neglected actually.'

'I can't think why. She's got a whole houseful of people looking after her.'

'I'll send her down. We'll be down for lunch in a while.' Wisely, he decided against telling his mother of the disgraceful behaviour of the child in the kitchen.

'Goodness, where does time go to?' She went into the lounge to await her daughter. 'Hallo, dear. Have you had a nice morning?'

'Not really. It's all right now you're here.'

'So what have you been doing?'

'Nothing. Paula made me sit quietly and read. I can't read properly so I pretended. It was very boring.'

Nellie listened to her daughter's

words and decided she needed to speak to her daughter-in-law. It wasn't good enough, and she was a teacher after all. The lunch gong sounded and she breathed a sigh of relief. She actually felt rather hungry, having missed her breakfast. 'Come along now, dear. Go and wash your hands ready for lunch.'

Bella did as she was told and went into the downstairs cloakroom. She left the tap running quite gently and gave a giggle to herself. That would teach them.

'Would you carve, dear?' Nellie asked William. 'You'd better sit in your father's place.' He hesitated and moved over.

'Doesn't really seem right,' he muttered. He carved the meat carefully, serving each of them with a hefty portion. Sarah carried the plates round to the three females and then left them to it. Conversation was rather sparse as they all ate, none of them wanting to mention James and how he might be getting on. When they finished the main course, Sarah cleared away and then brought in a large pie. Again, William served it, feeling a strange new responsibility falling on his shoulders.

'I want you to go to see your father this afternoon, William,' Nellie said.

'I want to go too,' Bella said.

'I'm sorry dear, but you can't.'

'I want to go. I want to go. Where is he, anyway?'

'I told you. He's in hospital and he is very poorly.'

'Why?'

'It's just something that happens when you get older. Now, eat up your pudding and be good.'

'Can I go into the hospital at any time?' William asked his mother.

'Oh yes, I think so. Under the circumstances, they won't mind at all.'

'I think I'll go too,' Paula suggested.

'Really, dear? I thought you might help out with Bella. I have some work I need to do.'

Paula sighed. She hated to be used as a babysitter, especially with the wretched Bella.

'Actually, I'd really like Paula to come with me,' William told Nellie. Paula could have kissed him. 'If that's all right with you, of course.'

'Oh well, all right. If that's what you want. I suppose Bella will be fine with me.'

'I'm sure she'll benefit from some time spent with you,' Paula told her. She left it at that and said no more, avoiding Nellie's slightly puzzled look.

They set off for the hospital as soon as they'd finished lunch. Paula couldn't help remembering the days when she had travelled to the same hospital by bus after school. Her mother had had cancer and she had feared the worst. However, she now seemed remarkably fit, all things considered.

Mr Cobridge was in a private room and there had been no change since he'd been there. He was attached to several pipes to help with his breathing and to monitor him.

'I wonder if there's anyone we can ask about him?' Paula said.

'Sure to be,' William replied. 'Even on a Sunday there will be someone on duty. Let's go and see. There's a nurse over there.'

They asked if they could see a doctor and were told to go back to Mr Cobridge's room. Someone would come to see them soon. They sat awkwardly on the chairs provided and spoke a little to each other. William was concerned about his father's state and said as much to his wife.

'Hush. He may be able to hear you,' she whispered.

'I don't think so. Not really.'

'Let's not take any chances. Oh, here comes someone now.'

'Mr Cobridge?' said the doctor. 'I'm Doctor Anderson. I'm looking after your father. How do you do.'

'How do you do. So how is he? Really, I mean.'

'He's not very good. I have to admit, we're all rather concerned. He should have come round by now but he still seems to be unconscious.'

'So do you think he's going to come round?' asked Paula.

'We have every hope he will, at some point. Remaining in his current state isn't entirely a bad thing. It allows his body to repair some of the damaged tissues.'

'But he looks so poorly,' Paula said without thinking.

'I'm not trying to make light of it. He is very ill. We're hoping he'll pick up in the next few days.'

'Thank you, Doctor,' William spoke, his voice somewhat choked. 'Is there anything we can do in the meantime?'

'I'm afraid it's a matter of biding our time. We hope things will improve in the next day or two. I don't know if you pray, but perhaps you could do that. There's not much point in you staying here, unless you want to of course. We do understand that Mr Cobridge is an important man in the community, and we'll do our best for him.'

'Thank you. We may as well go back home now. Don't you agree, Paula?'

'Whatever you think is best, love.'

'You'll let us know of any changes? I think you have the phone number.'

The doctor looked at his notes. 'Indeed, yes. And don't worry. He'll be well looked after.'

The two of them left the bedside and walked along corridors that were all too familiar to Paula. They said very little as they drove home, and William looked for Nellie when they arrived. She was sitting by the fire, looking as if she hadn't moved in ages. Bella was nowhere to be seen.

'Mother? Are you all right?'

'How is he?'

'No change I'm afraid. We spoke to the doctor and he said it's a matter of waiting. They'll phone if there's any change. Now, have you had some tea? I'll ring the bell for Sarah to bring some up, shall I?'

Nellie nodded. 'Cups of tea will solve any problem, won't they?' she muttered inconsequentially.

'Where's Bella?'

'I don't know. Perhaps she went to the kitchen. She seems to like it there.' William raised his eyebrows to Paula. After this morning's episode with the flour, he could imagine how Cook felt about having her there. Still, it was nothing to do with him.

The next few days were rather tense. Paula went to school and Bella seemed somewhat subdued. Nellie went to the factory each day, trying to do her best to keep up with James's appointments. William took over some of Nellie's duties and actually enjoyed himself. He had only dealt with a few of the 'girls' in the decorating department, those who were working on his special projects, but now he worked with more of them. Whenever the phone rang, he rushed to take the call, but there was nothing further from the hospital. They had also taken to dining with Nellie in the evenings, not wanting her to feel quite so alone. Paula was never quite sure how Nellie felt about this, but went along with her husband and quite enjoyed not having to think of things to cook. It was never very easy to chatter, but at least they knew they were helping her a little.

It was Thursday morning when the call came. Nellie was at work as usual, and William just happened to be in his father's office with his mother.

'Mrs Cobridge? I'm so sorry to have tell you that Mr Cobridge has died without recovering consciousness.' Nellie went white and looked as if she was about to faint. William rushed forward to take the phone out of her hands.

'Hallo? It's William Cobridge here.'

'Oh, yes. I'm very sorry to say, your father has died without regaining consciousness.'

'But he can't have done. You said he'd be better after a few days.'

'I'm so sorry. He didn't really improve at all and then he just slipped away.'

'I'll come in. Right away. Thank you, Doctor.' He put the phone down and turned to his mother. 'I'm going to the hospital right away. Do you want to come?'

'I suppose I should. Oh yes, of course I will. I want to see him once more. Oh James. How could you do this to me? Why did you have to leave me like this?'

'I'm so sorry, Mother. Come on. Let's go.'

The following days were very difficult. Nellie seemed to have lost all her fire. The funeral arrangements fell mostly on William. The factory was to be closed for the day to allow the workers to attend the service, and various friends from the past years would also be present. They decided to have a small, quiet wake at Cobridge House for just the family and one or two close friends. William made the arrangements with the cook to provide sandwiches and he organised drinks. He felt himself floundering somewhat as he didn't know what might be expected. He asked his mother for her advice but she simply brushed it off, telling him to do as he liked.

The day before the funeral, Nellie seemed to come to life again. 'I must find something to wear,' she announced. 'I need a smart outfit and yes, a new hat. Can you take me to Huntbach's, dear?' she asked William.

'What today?'

'Of course today. I need it for tomorrow. I can't let James down now, can I?'

'I suppose not. I'll take you this afternoon. I have things to do this morning.'

'Don't be silly, dear. There's nothing more important that your father's funeral. I need to go right away in case Huntbach's don't have anything suitable. We'll need to go elsewhere.'

William sighed. Paula had already left for school and had taken Bella with her. She was to have the day off the next day for the funeral but was working till the last minute.

'I must make a phone call, and then I'll be ready to take you.'

'We'll go in the Bentley. I suppose it's now mine. I'll go and get ready.'

William made two phone calls and hoped he'd sorted out the two meetings he'd had scheduled for the day. After all, his mother came first and was the most important person to be pacified for the coming days. He was certainly not looking forward to sitting near the changing rooms, waiting for his mother to choose some outfit. They drove away from Cobridge House and arrived in Hanley. He stopped the car outside the store and told his mother he'd find somewhere to park and be back for her later.

'Nonsense, dear. Leave it here. Nobody will mind under the circumstances.' She got out and stood waiting for her son. 'Come on. I'll have a word with doorman.'

With a shrug, William got out and followed her into the store.

'I'm leaving my car outside for a while,' Nellie said. 'I need to be dressed for my husband's funeral tomorrow.' And she swept through to the ladieswear department. William followed her, feeling like a tame puppy. He glanced back at the doorman, who was gazing after them in amazement.

'I hope you're right, Mother,' he muttered as she made her progress through the store. She didn't look at the racks of clothes but went straight for the lady who seemed to be in charge.

'I need a dress and coat for my husband's funeral tomorrow. And a hat,' she added.

'Certainly, madam. What sort of style?'

'Oh, I don't know. Something suitable. Bring me some things to look at.' She sat herself down and waited. William stood awkwardly to one side, wishing himself anywhere other than here.

Nellie was very particular about the clothes she was brought.

'I don't like the beads on that one.'

'Not that one. It looks as if I'm trying to be too young.'

'Haven't you got anything more suitable?'

'We do have one outfit that might suit,' said the slightly exasperated woman. 'It's quite expensive though. One of the leading designers, don't you know.'

'I thought I'd made it clear that cost is unimportant. Bring this creation to me.' Nellie was adamant. 'Ah yes, that is more like it. I'll try it on.' She picked herself up and went into the changing rooms.

William glanced at his watch. Unbelievably, it was after midday. His mother was in the fitting rooms for what seemed an eternity. He still wasn't sure why he'd had to bring her. Surely the gardener could have brought her here. He smiled to himself at the thought of their gardener standing here. Not quite the right scene for him. At last Nellie emerged, dressed in the clothes she had come in.

'They're going to alter it for me. I said you'd come back to collect it before they close.'

'Can't they send it over to the house?'

'Not today. I need to have it there ready for tomorrow. You don't mind, do you? Of course not. Come on then. We need to go to the factory now.'

He gave a shrug and followed his mother out of the shop. The car was still where he'd left it, amazingly, and they got in and he drove away.

'Good. A job well done. Now, have you got your dark suit and a black tie?'

'I suppose so.'

'Not good enough, dear. Stop somewhere and we'll get you a new tie. And you must have a new white shirt too.'

'I'll pick them up when I go to collect your outfit. Now please can we get back to work? I have a million things to do. Do you want me to drop you back at home?'

'Of course not. I have to run the factory now. I've had enough time off.'

'Fine.' William felt exhausted. He was plagued by the thought of what might happen in future. Would he rise to be chairman of the firm, or would that role stay with his mother? If she became chairman, who would take over her role in the decorating management? Whatever his worries, they had to get through the next couple of days.

At five-thirty, he set off back to Hanley. He'd left rather late, as he'd been busily making sure everything was ready to close down for the following day. The ovens were filled and ready to be fired but were left unlit until the following evening, when the men would come in to do it. It would mean their output was affected but with some overtime, they would certainly catch up the following week. He was held up in the busy traffic and arrived almost as the store was closing. He ran to the ladieswear department and asked for Nellie's outfit.

'I'm sorry, sir, but it's not quite finished. My girls will stay late to work on it.'

'Oh lord. How long will it be?'

'Half an hour at most, sir. Can I get you some tea?'

'No, thanks. I'll go to menswear and collect myself a shirt.'

'I'm afraid we're already cashed up, sir.'

'They'll have to put it on Mother's

account. I must have a new shirt and a black tie.'

After much phoning and humming and muttering, a shirt and tie were brought to him. He signed the chit and it was packed into a bag. At last his mother's outfit was brought to him, and he grabbed it and set off home. He slumped into an armchair when he finally got back to their apartment.

'Had a bad day, love?' asked Paula.

'Let's just forget all about it. I suppose we have to go down for dinner, do we?'

'I'm afraid so. Once tomorrow's over, we'll settle back into our routine.'

'I hope you've got something suitable to wear tomorrow? If not, I'll paint you black and that will have to do.'

'Don't worry. I do have something. I really don't understand why your mother needed a whole new outfit though. She has loads of black things she could have worn.'

'Don't ask. I'm never sure of my mother's motives for anything.'

5

By Thursday evening, Nellie was exhausted. She had entered her full widow's role and spoken to everyone at the funeral and then back at the house, and had entertained the people who had returned with the close family. Nobody was supposed to have come back with the main mourners, but many people had. Cook had done an amazing job in preparing food for everyone, despite the extra guests who turned up. Lizzie had stayed on when everyone else had gone.

'Are you all right, Nellie?' she asked.

'I'm fine. I'm anxious to see what James said in his will but then, I'll have to do whatever he's instructed.'

'What do you mean? Obviously he'll have left it all to you.'

'I don't know. William's been working hard lately and he may have been left a share in the factory. I'm going to see James's solicitor tomorrow, so not much longer to wait.'

'I'm so sorry. It was all rather sudden. But you must be cheered by all the people who came to the service.'

'Well, I did give them all the day off, so I expected a good turn out.'

'It was nice to see Vera again, wasn't it?'

'Oh yes. And some of the girls I used to work with. I did think Vera looked as if she'd aged quite a bit.' Vera had been in charge of the decorating shop at the factory for many years and had now retired. Nellie gave a sigh. 'I feel exhausted. Do you want a cuppa?'

'Go on then. Shall I ring the bell?' Lizzie went across to the fireplace and pressed the button alongside it. 'Sit yourself down before you drop.'

'I will, love. Thanks for staying on.'

'Where's William?'

'He's gone to the factory. Said something about wanting to check the kilns before they fired them up.'

'He's a good lad, isn't he? Despite

what you thought of him when he was growing up.' But Nellie was staring into the fire and seemed not to have heard anything her sister was saying. 'Nellie?' Lizzie repeated.

'I'm sorry. What were you saying?'

'Nothing that matters. Maybe I should leave you now. Let you have a well-deserved rest. Besides, Daniel will be wondering where I am.'

'I'm frightened, Lizzie. I don't know what's going to happen next.'

'Come on, Nellie. You're never afraid of anything.'

'I've never been left on my own before. James has always been there for me . . . with me. We've made our decisions about everything together. Admittedly, lately he's been spending a lot of time in his office both here and at the factory. I'm not sure what he's been doing but I always assumed he was doing it in the interests of the business. Now it's all down to me.'

'And William,' Lizzie added.

'Oh, I don't know how much he's

really involved. He's done well with his plates and coronation stuff, but I'm not sure how much he knows about the rest of the factory. And times aren't particularly easy at present. Still, I'll have to see what the solicitor says.'

'Is William going with you?'

'I don't know. I never thought about it.'

'I think he should go with you. After all, it's his future too, isn't it?'

'I suppose so. Where's Sarah with that tea?'

'I'd better get off. I'll call in at the kitchen on my way out and send her up with some for you.'

'Thanks, Lizzie. Enjoy your evening. Bye, dear.' The sisters kissed each other and Lizzie swept out, leaving Nellie feeling more alone than she would have believed.

* * *

At the factory, William walked through the empty rooms, thinking hard. He half-expected to inherit at least some of the factory, but then Nellie might have been left the whole thing. He didn't quite know how he felt about it. Scared? Apprehensive? Excited? All of those things. He went up to his father's office and looked around. It was very neat and tidy, with a pile of Potteries magazines lying on top of his desk. He flicked through some of them. There was an advert for Cobridge china on one page. It looked good, but he wondered about the future. His future.

He went downstairs and outside to the yard where the kilns stood waiting. He glanced at his watch. Where were the men who were supposed to be coming in to light them? He'd need to have a word with them, especially if they failed to turn up.

'All right, sir?' called a voice.

'Oh good, you're here.'

'All set to go. Be a good thing when we finally lose these old giants,' said Jake. He was a fireman from way back and was almost ready to retire.

'True enough. I'm hoping we're nearing the end of wood-fired kilns. Once we've got all the electric kilns out here, as well for decorated pieces, you'll be out of a job.'

'Can't say I'll miss it. I'm getting a bit past it now.'

'I'm sure. Is anyone else here with you?'

'Couple of the lads are round the other side. Do you know who'll be in charge in future?'

'Not sure yet. Everything will go on as normal for the time being. I'll leave you to it.'

'Okay, sir. No worries. We'll soon have this old girl fired up and working for us.'

William nodded and left the area. He went out to his car and drove himself back to Cobridge House, deep in thought. He desperately needed to talk things through with Paula. How would she feel about moving more into the family circle? He felt they were still relatively newlyweds and she would probably want to stay in her own part of the house. So much would depend on what his mother wanted them to do.

Nellie was waiting to see him and called him into the drawing room. 'I'd like you to come to see the solicitor with me tomorrow,' she said. 'My appointment is at eleven o'clock. You can drive me in the Bentley.'

'Very well, Mother. Eleven o'clock, you say? That will give me time to go into work earlier and see that everything is moving on as it should.'

'I'll come in with you. I need to look at James's desk. Get some idea of what he's been doing lately. Make sure I'm continuing along the same line.'

'Very well. What time do you want to leave?'

'Eight-thirty, as usual. I take it Paula will take Bella to school.'

'I suppose so. Or we could drop her off on our way?'

'The walk will do her good. I don't want her to become reliant on always being driven in.'

'I'll ask Paula. Now if there's nothing else, I'll go up and see my wife.'

'Oh, I thought you'd both have dinner with me.'

'All right. I'll still go and talk to Paula. We'll be down at seven-thirty as usual.' He leapt up the stairs and went into the apartment. 'I'm here Paula.'

'Oh thank goodness. Bella is driving me mad. Is Nellie downstairs?'

'She's sitting in the drawing room.'

'Good. She can have some time with her daughter. Bella, your mother's downstairs. Go down and see her now.'

'Shan't. She doesn't want me anyway.'

'Come on. I'll go down with you. You need to be quiet with her. She's feeling rather sad.' William was firm with his sister and took her hand and led her downstairs to join his mother. He almost pushed her into the room and left her there. It was less than half an hour before they were summoned down again and he desperately wanted to speak to Paula.

'Mother wants us to join her for

dinner again,' he told her. 'I hope you don't mind too much.'

'Oh dear. I really hoped for a quiet evening up here. Just the two of us.'

'I know, but well, she did almost insist. We won't let it become an unbreakable habit. Still, it does mean you don't have to cook. Look on that as a benefit.'

'Oh don't worry. And you're right, it does save me from cooking and shopping. I don't really mind. Cook is much better than I am, anyway.'

'Mother is also relying on you to take Bella to school tomorrow. I'm sorry, but she was very firm in not wanting her to rely on a lift to school.'

Paula looked at him crossly. She felt annoyed by Nellie's attitude to her and treating her as a baby-sitter. 'Well all right but again, I'm not prepared to take her on permanently. Just until your mother knows what she's doing with the business. I'm not sure how to tell her that, but I hope she'll understand.'

'Mother's asked me to drive her to

the solicitor's tomorrow. I'm not sure what the terms of my father's will are. It's all a bit difficult, isn't it?'

'I'm sorry, love. Indeed, it is difficult. Do you think you'll be mentioned in it?'

'I suppose I must be, if only as Nellie's eventual successor. Come on, let's get ready for dinner. Are you changing, or going like that?'

'I'm going like this.' She was still dressed in mourning clothes. 'It seems more appropriate for today.'

*   *   *

At eleven o'clock the following day, Nellie and William sat in the solicitor's office awaiting their fate. It seemed the will had been written some time ago and had not been updated for over three years. William thought back and realised he was still in his travelling mode back then. That must mean he wouldn't be mentioned as a successor.

The solicitor read out his father's words. 'To my beloved wife Nellie, I leave the factory and all my assets. I trust she will continue to work there and to drive the business in the way I have done for so many years. Should she pre-decease me, then I leave the company to my son William George Cobridge and trust that he will seek advice in managing it.'

Nellie breathed a sigh of relief. At least she now knew it was down to her to take the factory forward. William could continue to do as he had been doing and she would support him as much as she could. And Cobridge House remained in her possession. That was also something of a relief.

'Thank you very much,' Nellie said to the solicitor. 'I suppose I must make a will myself now. I'll be in touch soon.' They passed a few pleasantries and left. William looked at his mother and congratulated her. He didn't mean to sound bitter but he did feel somewhat left out.

'So, where to now?' he asked.

'Back to the factory of course. I have

a great deal of work to do. I need to see all of your father's papers and see what deals there are in the pipeline.'

'Let me know if I can help at all.'

'Oh, I will. Meanwhile, you get on with the coronation memorabilia. I'm expecting it to make us a lot of money. It's a limited market and won't last for long.'

'You're quite right, Mother. It won't last for long.' He remained silent for a while and then, taking a deep breath, plunged in. 'What are you going to do about Bella?'

'Bella? What on earth has she got to do with anything?'

'You can't rely on Paula to act as a baby-sitter, you know. She is very fed up with the way she behaves and sees quite enough of her at school.'

'Don't be silly, dear. Paula doesn't mind, surely?'

'I think she does. You have no idea how difficult the child is. I think Cook is also fed up with her being in the kitchen. You need to get someone to come in and look after her, or do some more of it yourself.'

'You are being silly, dear. She's a perfectly normal little girl. A bit full of high spirits, but Paula should be well able to cope with her.' Nellie clearly wanted nothing more to do with it. William had done his best, and with no results he could report to his wife. Maybe it was time for them to look for a place of their own. That way, she would be spared from her duties as unpaid baby-sitter. They could afford it, at least. He'd managed to save reasonably well from his salary, and Paula was earning too. He made up his mind to discuss it with her.

Nellie seemed to have her impetus back. She swept into the factory and went straight to her husband's office. She called his secretary and told her the news. 'I want a memo sent out to all staff to say I am now in charge and will be visiting all departments in the next week or so. And I'd love some tea.'

'Very well, Missus Nellie. I suppose I

can still call you that?'

'Of course. In private, of course.' The woman left her and Nellie took out the bunch of keys and opened William's desk. There were various things in his drawer. His work diary for one thing. She looked through it for the next few days. He had several meetings scheduled, which she needed to address. One problem was the venue. He had set them up at his club and this would have to be changed. She was not allowed to enter the doors of such places. She would invite them to come to the factory. After all, his office was perfectly respectable and it would save money too. His subscription to the club for a start. She looked at his bank statements and was quite horrified to see the amount of money he spent on entertaining clients. This would stop immediately. James had been far too indulgent with his friends. No wonder he had been putting on weight at such a rate. It had cost him his life in the end, or at least contributed to his demise.

The secretary came in with her tea. 'I've put some biscuits on a plate. Mister James used to like some chocolate ones when he had tea.'

'Thank you, but I won't be needing them in future. I don't eat biscuits anyway.'

'Do you want to dictate your letter to the staff?'

'I'm sure you can prepare a brief statement along the lines I said to you. Let me see it before you duplicate it.'

'Certainly, ma'am. I'll do it right away.' Nellie smiled at her and thanked her. She rather liked the title 'ma'am'.

★   ★   ★

The day drew to its close for Paula. It had been a long, hard slog to her, with Bella behaving very badly. And it wasn't over yet. She had to take the child home and probably take her up to the apartment and look after her until Nellie returned, whatever time that would be. She was prepared to do it for now, but she needed to get something sorted out for the future. She wondered how the meeting at the solicitor's had gone. Presumably Nellie had inherited the factory, but hopefully William had been acknowledged too.

'Come along, Bella,' she told the child. 'Put your coat on and we'll walk home.'

'Will Daddy be back yet?' she asked.

'I'm afraid not, dear. He died and was buried yesterday. Don't you remember?'

'I thought he was coming back. Where is he now?'

'He has a grave at the church. He did come back yesterday before they all went to the church to bury him.'

'What do you mean? He was planted in the ground like daffodil bulbs?'

'Sort of.'

'Then he'll grow in the ground and come back like a baby.' She giggled at the prospect. 'It'll be funny when he does come back and I shall be older than he is.'

Wearily Paula let the subject drop. Her mother could sort out Bella's misconceptions. All she wanted to do was to get home and sit with her feet up. Maybe she would let Bella go and pester the cook.

William was late home, having had to wait for his mother. Hopefully, in future she would drive her own car into work and he could use his. He ran upstairs to the apartment and his waiting wife.

'How did it go at the solicitor's?' she asked as soon as he came in.

'As expected. Everything goes to Mother. The house and all his assets, as well as the factory. I'm not surprised at all. The will was written when I was in America, or even before. I was hardly a decent chap to leave anything to.'

'I'm sorry, love. I know you were hoping for at least a part-share.'

'I was thinking. I wonder if we shouldn't look for a place of our own?'

'Really?' she said in surprise. 'I thought you liked it here.'

'Oh I do. But well, Mother is

expecting you to look after Bella almost all the time. Take and bring her home from school, and look after her till she gets home.'

'Oh no. There are limits to the dutiful daughter-in-law.'

'Exactly. So what do you think?'

'It sounds like a plan. If I wasn't here, she'd have to get someone in to look after the child. Let's put it to her and see what she says. I must say, it would be rather nice. But can we afford it?'

'Well I reckon so. You're earning money too, so we won't be scraping the barrel.'

'Is she expecting us for dinner this evening?'

'I'm not sure. She didn't say anything as we drove home. But she was in a funny mood. All a bit high-powered in a way. It's almost as if she doesn't want anyone to think she's incapable of running the show.'

'Perhaps you'd better go and ask her. If not, I can easily make something. At least it's Friday and we have a weekend ahead to recover a bit.'

'It's been quite a week. I'll go and ask if we're expected downstairs.'

Paula watched him go. He was a bit upset about there being no mention of him in his father's will. But then, nothing had changed in reality. She still felt on the periphery of the family. They were all friendly enough, but they didn't live all that close by. She thought about her and William having somewhere of their own to live. It was quite an idea, but somehow she couldn't see it happening. After all the work that had been done to make the apartment habitable, she couldn't see Nellie welcoming the idea at all. But getting someone to look after Bella was a must.

'We're off the hook for dinner,' William told her when he came upstairs again.

'That's good. I didn't really feel like making polite conversation. Shall I open a tin of something?'

'Or how about I take you somewhere

nice for dinner?'

'That sounds wonderful. But it's rather late, isn't it?'

'I'll make a call. Go and put on your glad rags and we'll go and eat.'

'I really don't mind. We could go tomorrow instead,' she said. 'I do feel pretty weary actually.'

'Just as you like. Tomorrow it is. We'll go somewhere new. What have we got for now?'

'I'll dig into the cupboard and see what I can find.'

6

Over the following weeks, William was working hard. He had already acquired a large number of orders for his coronation plates. He wanted to be involved in other things too, and kept up a relentless campaign to get his mother to agree to his taking over the decorating shop. But she remained stubborn about what she considered to be her own personal area. She had begun her life in the industry there and wanted to keep it as her own thing.

'But Mother, you can't do everything. You're now involved in all the stuff Father used to do and want to keep this moving on too. Why not ease up on your responsibilities a bit and allow someone else to take over a few things?'

'It's possibly the most important part of the whole business. You've done well with your plates and things, but I'm the one who's kept everything else moving along. No, William, you're not yet ready for this responsibility.'

He left her office angrily and went to his own room. Nellie had taken over James's office and her old room was currently vacant. However, William was not allowed to use it. Instead, he was working in a tiny room at one side of the main offices. It was actually smaller than Nellie's secretary's office. He hated it and felt very much the underdog. He was unappreciated and knew it. He even wondered whether he should look for another job. Surely his family background would make him a desirable proposition for another company? He picked up some of the Potteries magazines and turned to the back, where local jobs were advertised. There were several that might interest him, though most of them seemed to expect someone older than him. Still, it was worth thinking about, and he made a note of the two best ones. It would certainly teach his mother not take him for granted. He lifted the phone and asked the operator to put him through to an estate agent.

That evening, he had some news for his wife. 'I've asked the estate agent to send me some information about properties in the area. I thought it might be nice to have a look at least. What do you think?'

'Oh William, how exciting. Where are they?'

'I don't know yet. I asked them to send stuff to me. Anything suitable really, within our price bracket.'

'And what do you think your mother will say?'

'Not sure. I'm really not bothered. She's taken it all on herself to run the factory and do everything. She won't even listen to me. And I'm still stuck in a tiny office when there's a large one available. I've even got some details of other jobs I might apply for.'

'My goodness, you certainly have got the bit between your teeth. Nellie isn't going to like all this change one little bit.'

'Well, she's brought it on herself. She refuses to let anything go. I'm in charge of the coronation stuff and that's all I'm allowed to do. It's a good job it's selling well or I suspect I'd be out of a job anyway. She's working herself into the ground and I know she can't keep it up. Not at this pace anyway.'

'Then don't rattle too many cages at once. She probably does rely on you more than you think.'

'I don't see it myself. Oh well. What's for dinner?'

'I've made a pie. Spared from Bella for once, I decided to cook something nice. It's my mother's recipe so it should be all right.'

'I do love you, Paula. I'm sorry to be such a grump.'

'I love you too. But we need to be a bit more sympathetic to your mum. She's lost the love of her life, don't forget. She's taken on your father's duties as well as her own. It's a big company she's looking after. Lots of people are relying on her to keep things

going. Now, let's forget about everything and enjoy our meal.'

*   *   *

Nellie sat downstairs with a tray. She
picked at the delicious meal before her
and thought about the past. James would
have hated the way she was eating. She
gazed around at the room. The huge
china cabinet was looking slightly grubby
and several things hadn't been dusted
properly for a while. She had never got
another maid in to help and Cook seemed
to have forgotten about her request. Sarah
had put Bella to bed and didn't complain
about the extra duties she had taken on
since James's death. One day soon she
would regain control of her home, but
for now it would do as it was. She felt
exhausted and wanted only to go to bed,
ready to be up early for the next day.

'Have you finished, Missus Nellie?'
said Sarah as she came into the room.

'Yes, thank you. I can't finish it, I'm
afraid.'

'I'll bring your dessert in.'

'No, I don't think I want anything else.'

'But Cook's made you summat special. Won't you try it?'

'I said no, thank you. Now take this back to the kitchen and leave me in peace.'

With a sigh, Sarah picked up the tray and took it to the kitchen. 'She don't want no pudding. And she's hardly touched this anyway. We might as well not have bothered,' Sarah told the cook. 'Honestly, she's got so thin it's painful to look at her.'

'She'll get over it one day soon, I don't doubt. Maybe a family get-together would be good for her. I'll maybe suggest it to her. One Sunday soon. We haven't had one of them for ever so long.'

'Good luck with that idea. I don't think she's interested in owt but the factory.'

Nellie took out some papers from her briefcase, the one James had used for several years, and started to work on them. Very soon she let them slip off her knee as she fell into a deep sleep. By the time she awoke, it was almost three o'clock in the morning. She felt stiff and uncomfortable and stretched as if it might waken her properly. She picked up the papers and cast her eyes over them. The figures danced in front of her eyes and she decided to go up to her bed. This was the third time she'd fallen asleep like this and it certainly wouldn't do. She needed to get some help and made the decision right there and then to get someone to come in and help with the management of the factory. She would draft an advertisement tomorrow and place it in the *Potteries Gazette*. She needn't say who it was with, and arrange interviews in a hotel somewhere. Feeling greatly relieved, she went to bed and managed to fall asleep immediately.

'You feeling better today?' asked Cook when she brought Nellie's breakfast to her.

'I am. I slept really well, thank you.'

'Dunno how that was. You were

snoring your head off when we went up to bed. I thought of waking you but decided you'd probably sleep better where you was. Any road, eat up your breakfast. And don't even think of leaving it.'

'I won't,' Nellie replied with a grin. She felt hungry and tucked into the bacon and eggs with relish. It was a turning point in her life, she decided.

'I was thinking,' said Cook. 'It's about time we had a family do. How about inviting them all over at the weekend? Sunday tea always goes down well.'

'Oh not this weekend coming. I need to relax a bit. Perhaps the following one?'

'Right. I'll leave it to you to invite them all. I'll concentrate on the meal. It'll be like old times, having them all here.'

'Not quite like old times,' Nellie said sadly.

'No, well you're right of course. But nearly like old times. I'll get some beer delivered and we'll get some wine up from the cellar. Haven't bin down there since . . . well, since the funeral.'

'I need to see what there is down there. Take stock. I'll do it at the weekend. Now, if you don't leave me alone, I'll never finish all this food.'

In her office, Nellie spent the first half hour drafting her advertisement for an assistant manager. When she was satisfied, she typed it herself and put it into an envelope. The fewer people who knew about it, the better. She felt pleased with it and had decided to use an agency. She planned to send them her draft and then leave it to them to make a shortlist of people she would interview later. She then got on with her normal day, happy in the thought that she might soon have someone to share her burden. She put the letter in her handbag, intending to post it later.

There was a knock at her door. 'Are you ready for some tea?' asked her secretary.

'Oh yes, please.' She glanced at the clock. It was already almost ten o'clock.

'Goodness, how time flies by. I'll look at the post next.'

When that was finished, Nellie decided to go on a tour of the factory. She wanted to make sure everything was moving along properly and in any case, it did the workers good to see the boss regularly.

'Do you want me to come with you? Make notes?' asked the secretary.

'Of course not. Why would I?'

'Mister James used to ask me to make notes on the rare occasions he went round.'

'I see. Well, I don't need you with me, thank you. You can do the replies to the morning's post.'

'Very well, ma'am.' She was obviously put out, Nellie thought. Still, it was the woman's job to be her secretary and she could jolly well do it how Nellie wanted. If James had treated her differently, then it was up to him. She was in charge now.

She set out on her tour. Down at the clay end she saw her brother Ben, up to his armpits in clay, as usual. He was a fine potter and made jugs and other hand-thrown pots.

'Hallo, our Nellie. How you doing?'

'I'm fine, thanks. Just having a wander round to see how things are going. How are your little ones? And Jenny?'

'They're lovely, ta. How about you and yorn?'

'Fine, thanks. Look, I'm thinking of having a family tea a week on Sunday. I hope you'll come?'

'Thanks, Nellie. It'll be good to see everyone again. We haven't met up since the . . . well, since the funeral. You are doing all right, aren't you?'

'I'm fine, thanks, Ben. Very busy though. Must get on. I see you're still making some good stuff. Keep it up.'

'I'm doing some stuff for William. Some ideas he's got for the coronation stuff.'

'I see. I'll speak to him about it later. See you next week.'

'All reet, love. I'll tell Jenny and the kids. They'll love to come over. Always do.'

She walked through the casting shop and stopped to speak to the manager. 'Everything on schedule?' she asked.

'Fine, thanks, missus. I'm busy with William's plates. Got four of my workers on them. The rest are doing the usual stuff. Been a bit quiet on the decorating front, so I'm just stockpiling at present.'

'I wonder why?' Nellie asked.

'Dunno. Expect they'll pick up again soon.'

'Right, I'll go there next. Find out what's going on.'

She bypassed the gloss department and went straight to the decorating shop. The main man in the department seemed to be in conference with her son and she walked into his office, interrupting the flow of conversation.

'Morning. Or is it afternoon?'

'Morning, Missus Nellie.' He spoke reasonably respectfully. 'How are you today?'

'Fine, thank you. I hear the orders are a little slow at present?'

'Well, apart from the coronation stuff, yes they are. People aren't buying china the way they used to.'

'Hmm, I wonder why that is? Haven't you got any new lines to show them?'

'Not really. We don't have a chief designer anymore. Not since you left to take over the factory. And there isn't a proper manager either. I've been bumbling along trying my best, but I'm not a manager.'

'I've been telling you this for a while,' said William, listening to the words.

'I'll look into it. I want to look round and see what they're working on.' Nellie turned away from the two men and set off along the decorating shop. She paused to look at the girls' work. She was pleased to see some of them were working on her designs. 'You're doing well, ladies,' she said as she stopped at one of the benches. 'Keep the lines clean and neat.'

'Yes, miss,' one of the younger girls replied. Nellie left without correcting her.

As she walked along the other side, she saw that they were all working on coronation plates and mugs. She frowned slightly. They were all good, but she was irritated to see that so many staff were working on a single line.

'A word please, William,' Nellie snapped. 'Come into my office.' She walked back along the corridor with her son following. 'On whose authority have you taken over the entire decorating shop?'

'I'm sorry?' he blustered.

'I see you've taken over the majority of the shop to do your coronation stuff. I just hope it sells. You do realise what a small market it is? Time-limited too.'

'There was nothing else for them to do. I thought I'd be doing them a favour giving them something to do. Father was quite happy about what I was doing.' William was furious.

'Your father is no longer in charge. I am.'

'And don't we all know it,' he said.

'What do you mean by that?'

'Never mind. You've made it perfectly

clear that you're in charge. Do you want me to stop them from working on 'my stuff', as you call it?'

'I'll look at the order books and let you know. Go on now. Leave me to get on with my work.'

Saying nothing more, he turned and left the office. He was making up his mind to apply for one of the posts he'd seen. He simply wasn't appreciated here. He would see through the coronation memorabilia and then leave. He and Paula would find somewhere else to live and leave Cobridge House and the family behind them. It would cause no end of difficulties within the family, but he wasn't going to be treated like this.

Fortunately for him, the orders for his plates and mugs were coming in fast. Several local shops had sold their first cautious orders immediately and had ordered more. He ignored his mother's remarks and set the workers to make more. They were fired quickly in the new electric ovens and were ready to leave the factory in record

116

time. Feeling pleased with himself, he sent copies of the orders up to his mother. She said nothing to him directly but had made a note of what he had produced. She didn't like to be thought wrong about anything at all and merely gave a shrug.

On Sunday morning she phoned her brother Joe, and Lizzie, inviting them to come for tea the following weekend. 'With all the family, of course. I thought it was time we had a proper family get-together.' They all accepted and she told Cook. 'It was a good idea of yours,' she said.

'Thought it would do you good to see them all again. I'll plan a menu and let you see it.'

'Oh, no — whatever you do will be fine.'

'Very well. And you said you wanted to check down the cellar?'

'Indeed yes. I'll do it right away. Thank you for thinking of this. I'm feeling much better with something to look forward to.'

Nellie went down into the cellar. It was the first time in many years she'd ventured down there. It had always been James who went down to choose the wines, or perhaps one of the housekeepers. She looked at the racks of wine and wondered what they all were. There was another rack of spirits and port. She really ought to bring some of it upstairs to offer to guests. But then, she hadn't had any guests for a long time. Perhaps she could sell some of it. It was possibly quite expensive wine, and didn't it get more expensive the older it was? She liked the idea and made up her mind to see someone about selling a lot of it off. She would never use it and it was an asset that she could make use of.

She selected a couple of bottles and took them upstairs to be used. She had no idea of what they were and doubted any of the family would know any better. She had always left these things to her husband, who had a liking and knowledge of wine. She had drunk whatever he provided, and some of it

118

she really didn't care for.

'These will do for next week. I'm not sure what they are and I doubt my family will either.'

The *Potteries Gazette* came out the following week. Nellie glanced at the advert she had drafted. It appeared pretty much as she had specified.

Wanted. Assistant Manager to work in a family firm. Full order books. All usual departments. Must be willing to work long hours and have a good general knowledge of all processes in the pottery industry. Apply by letter giving details of experience and reasons for your application. Reply to Messrs Jerome and Co. Interviews in near future.

William also had a copy of the magazine. He read the advert and punched the air. This was the very job he had been waiting for. It would mean leaving his mother in the lurch, but it was too good an opportunity to miss. He immediately started putting together his letter of application. He wondered where the factory was situated. It might mean they needed to find somewhere else to live to be near enough to it. Perhaps the company would help with removal fees. His mind was already whirring, but he realised he needed to go and see how his work was progressing. He desperately wanted to talk to someone about the prospects but knew he would have to wait until the evening when he could talk to Paula.

It seemed a long day. He could hardly wait to leave, and rushed through to get away on time. He told Paula all about the job and read her what he'd written so far.

'You sound so keen,' she told him. 'Don't be too disappointed if you don't get an interview.'

'Whoever the company is, I'm exactly what they need. I've had so much experience recently. I've designed the coronation lines and brought them into production and yes, I've seen them through the entire process. I looked at the plates we already have in production, admittedly, but I've been responsible for making sure we had them all ready to decorate. And I've been in charge of the sales team. That's most important. I think this is our future. If we have to move house to be near the factory, well it gives us every excuse. I can't think there'll be any problems with that.'

'I hope it isn't too far away. I'd hate to give up my job at this school. Bella apart, I do love the job.'

'We'll be able to start thinking of our own family soon. This job could be the very start we need.'

'But I . . . well, maybe so. You are right. I can't go on working forever. I'm nearly twenty-six, after all.'

'Exactly. If we wait too much longer, you'll be drawing a pension.'

'Oh shut up, you. But I do wish you every bit of luck.'

They chatted for the rest of the evening and by the time they went to bed William had got the job, bought a new house, and they even had two children. Paula was slightly more cautious.

7

Paula and William were excused from Sunday lunch duties. They ate something in their own apartment. Nellie, for once, went into the kitchen to eat with the cook, Sarah and Bella. The kitchen was full of wonderful smells. Cook had really gone to town and cooked a whole ham, a tongue and a whole range of cakes. There were salads to go with the cooked meats and she had bought some nice bread.

'You've done us proud, Cook,' said Nellie. 'I'm sure they'll all enjoy it.'

'I 'ope so, Missus. There's beer in the sideboard and that wine you brought up. I 'opes as you've opened it. I know the master used to do summat with it.'

'You're right. Didn't he put it in the decanter?'

'Oh lordy, yes he did. Sarah, you go and get the decanters — and wash them properly, mind.'

'Right away.' She left them and went into the dining room. She had to look for them as they'd been put away in the depths of the sideboard. 'I've found 'em,' she announced proudly.

'I suppose I should consider having more dinner parties,' Nellie murmured. 'Seems a shame to waste all the things James had. Ah well. Now, is the table laid ready?'

'I think so,' said Sarah. 'P'raps you could take a look at it? There's quite a lot of you to sit round it nowadays. Joe and his wife and child. Ben and his wife and two children. Then there's miss — sorry, Missus Lizzie and her fella and their little 'un. Mister William and Paula. Oh, and you and Bella. That makes . . . ' she paused to count up on her fingers. 'Well, quite a lot.'

'I don't think Lizzie's little one will want to sit at the table,' Nellie said with a smile.

'I've laid him a place, otherwise there'd be thirteen. And we all know that's not lucky.'

'I see. Quite a collection of people we are now. Thank you for all you've done, ladies. I'll go and change now. Have you got some extra help coming in?'

'We thought as how we'd manage. It's all ready apart from mashing the tea. And you said as 'ow you didn't want us to serve.'

'Very well. I'm sure it will all be splendid.'

Nellie went up to her room and looked at her clothes. It wouldn't do to be seen in her brightest clothes, not so soon after James had left them, but she decided against wearing black. It did drain her so. On the other hand, purple was supposed to be sign of mourning, so she chose one of her smarter purple dresses. She really was feeling better and ready to face the world. She went to look for Bella and make sure she was dressed appropriately. She was in her room playing with her dolls.

'Bella dear, you must get ready for this afternoon's tea party.'

'Why?

'Because there are lots of people coming and you want to look nice, don't you?'

'Don't care. They're not coming to see me anyway.'

'Of course they are. Change into that nice dress hanging in your wardrobe. And go and wash your hands and face.'

'Shan't. Not going to.' She crept under her bed and there she stayed, despite Nellie's cajoling and finally demanding.

'Bella, come out. Immediately. You'll stay there all afternoon and you'll miss all the lovely food Cook has made.' The child giggled but stayed where she was. 'Very well. Stay there,' Nellie almost screamed at her daughter. She left the room and slammed the door. She did not understand what had got into the girl. She would discuss it with Jenny when she arrived. Perhaps she might have the answer. Paula seemed prejudiced about the child and constantly seemed to complain about her behaviour. For now Nellie had other problems, like who should she ask to carve the meat? William or Joe?

An hour later, the entire family had arrived. It was a bit like bedlam when they all were together, with the children and assorted adults. Nellie smiled at everyone and felt very happy to have her flock around her.

'Where's Bella?' asked Jenny.

'Hiding under her bed,' Nellie replied. 'At least, she was when I last saw her.'

'Why on earth would she do that?'

'I have no idea. I was hoping you might have some insight into the child and her behaviour. I know Paula has mentioned it a few times, but I've never known her to be so stubborn before.'

'Shall I go and see her?' asked the one-time nursery nurse.

'Would you, dear? I'd be very grateful.'

Jenny went upstairs to Bella's room. She knocked at the door and went in. 'Bella? Where are you?'

'Hallo, Jenny. I'm hiding.'

'Aren't you coming down to see the rest of the family?'

'Don't want to.'

'All right. I'll leave you here then. Bye.' She turned and left the room, waiting outside the door to see if Bella came out. After five minutes she gave up and went down to join the rest of the family.

'Sorry. She didn't want to come out. I left her there. She'll probably come down for tea.'

'Thank you anyway, dear. Now, I think it's about time we all went into the dining room. I think everything's ready. Paula dear, can you tell Cook we're ready for tea now?' Her daughter-in-law nodded and went through to the kitchen.

All the food was on the table ready, and they went into the dining room.

'Wow, this looks good,' said Joe.

'Not arf,' added Ben.

They all sat down, ready to eat their fill. Lizzie and Daniel had left their son in his carry cot until the meal was over. The other little ones sat at the table with cushions under them so they could reach. Everyone was beautifully behaved, and Nellie smiled benevolently round the table.

'Joe, would you like to carve the ham; and William, can you look after the tongue?' She had decided to ask both of them to do the honours. A large pork pie had also appeared on the table, and a dish of hard boiled eggs.

'Cor, it's like the old days sitting here,' said Joe. 'Oh, sorry, Nellie.'

'It's fine. I know what you mean though. Now, does anyone want tea? Or there's wine and beer.'

The tea party was going well, exactly as Nellie had hoped. Cook had done wonders and everyone ate and drank very well.

'I see Bella didn't join us,' remarked Ben. 'Doesn't she like family dos?'

'Evidently not,' Nellie said.

'Won't she miss out on tea then?' asked Daisy, Joe's wife.

'She'll probably go into the kitchen and pester Cook,' Paula commented. 'She usually does spend a lot of time there.'

'How's she doing at school?' asked Jenny.

'Not terribly well. Her behaviour leaves much to be desired.' Paula glanced at Nellie, not sure how her comments would go down. But her mother-in-law seemed not to have heard. She was talking to Lizzie and asking about their son.

It was about seven o'clock when some members of the family decided it was time to leave. 'The children are very tired, you know,' said Ben. 'Lovely party though. Thanks a lot, sis.'

'It's been lovely to see you all. Thank you for coming.'

Joe and his family and Ben and his family left almost immediately. Lizzie stayed on to talk to her sister. She felt concerned about Bella and asked why she had stayed in her room.

'I really don't know. Maybe she

didn't like having everyone here, as Jenny suggested. She always seems quite normal to me, but Paula says she doesn't behave well at school. Well, you may have heard what she said.'

'Can't she have some tests? There are lots of new ideas about what can be wrong with children these days.'

'I think Paula was looking into it. I must ask her where she's got to. I suppose with James's death, everything has ground to a halt. This is the first time I've felt anything like normal. I've also decided to appoint an assistant manager. It's all in hand.'

'Not William?' asked Daniel.

'Oh I don't think so. He's a bit too close to the family.'

'I'd have thought he'd be ideal. He knows the factory top to bottom and is very aware of all the problems.'

'Well, I've organised it all now. Jerome and company are going to make a shortlist for me.'

'Let me know if I can help at all, won't you?'

'Thank you, Daniel. Very kind of you. I rely on you very much you know, to keep us on the straight and narrow.' Lizzie's husband was in charge of the finances.

'William's doing very well with his coronation memorabilia,' Daniel told her. 'I've been very gratified to see his results.'

'That's good. It's such a limited market though. Once June is over, there'll be masses of stock piled up in the stores.'

'I somehow doubt that. William's been very strict about getting payments in, with deliveries. I think we're going to make quite some profit from his enterprise.'

'Good. I'm pleased to hear it. Perhaps he has got some idea of the business after all.'

'I think he'll be very upset if he doesn't get a shot at being assistant manager.'

'He's much too young. Now, Lizzie, do you want to feed Samuel before you go?'

'He'll be fine now, thanks. I suppose we should be leaving, don't you think, Daniel?'

'As you like, love. Thanks, Nellie. It's been great. I really like your Joe, you know. I had a very interesting talk with him about his cattle.'

'Come on,' said Lizzie impatiently. 'We don't want to hear about it now.'

Laughing, they got their things together and left. Nellie waved them off and went back inside. Paula and William had gone back to their apartment some time ago, so she sat in the drawing room, thinking about the afternoon. She felt a million miles away from Joe and Ben these days. Apart from there parentage, she felt they had nothing in common. Ben worked in the factory but she didn't really see much of him. She felt very guilty about her thoughts but assumed most families were like that. As for Lizzie, she was very wrapped up in her own family and didn't really have much time for anything else.

Nellie decided she really should go and thank Cook for her splendid efforts, and perhaps see where Bella was now. She rose and went along to the kitchen. Bella was sitting in state at the table, picking up bits from all the plates and stuffing them into her mouth.

'Now Miss Bella, that's not the way to eat,' said Sarah helplessly.

'Yes 'tis. I like eating this way.'

'If your mother sees you, she won't like it.'

Bella laughed. 'She can see me. She's there.' She stuffed a large piece of ham into her mouth and chewed it with her mouth open.

'Bella, really,' said Nellie, appalled at her daughter's behaviour. 'Behave yourself.'

'I like eating like this. I was hungry.' She reached for more meat and stuffed that into her mouth as well.

'Put the ham away please, Sarah. And the rest of the food. If she can't eat properly then she can do without. Go up to your room immediately, Bella. I'll follow you up there in a minute.'

'I hate you!' screamed the child. 'And you don't love me anymore. Or you wouldn't make me go to my room.'

'Go there now,' said Nellie coldly. She meant business and Bella leapt off her chair and ran out of the room. 'I'm sorry, Sarah. How long was she here?'

'Quite a while. I was clearing the table and left things here. She came in and started eating. I didn't quite know what to do.'

'What's wrong with your hand?' she asked, seeing a crude bandage on the maid's hand.

'Erm . . . well, I cut myself.'

'How did you do that?'

The maid blushed and looked away.

'It was Bella, wasn't it?' Nellie said in horror. 'Bella did it, didn't she?'

'Well, yes. But it was an accident. I tried to take the carving knife away from her and she sort of slashed out. I'm sorry, Missus Nellie.'

'Not at all. I'm very sorry too. I'll go

and sort her out in a minute. But I came to thank Cook. Where is she?

'She's in the sitting room. She's having a bit of a rest.'

'I'll have a word with her and then go and try to sort out my wretched daughter.' She knocked at the door and went into the little sitting room. 'I just came to thank you for a marvellous effort. They all enjoyed the meal and asked me to thank you.'

'Don't mention it. I enjoyed cooking some nice food for once. It's bin a bit quiet round 'ere lately.'

'I know. We'll soon be back to normal. I shall plan some dinner parties soon.'

'All reet. Will you be wantin' owt else tonight?'

'Oh no, I don't think so. You take it easy for the rest of the day. Sarah's putting things away. I may have a hot drink later. I'll ring if I want anything. I'd better go and see what Bella's doing now. Good night. And thank you again.'

She ran upstairs and went into

Bella's room. She was hiding under her bed again. Nellie was furious with her daughter and stood glaring.

'Get out from under there right away. Come on now.'

'No. I'm staying here. You're mean and nasty.'

'You have no idea how mean and nasty I can be. Come out immediately.'

'No.'

'Bella, I won't tell you again. One, two ... ' The child crept out from under the bed and stood looking defiant. 'What do you mean by attacking Sarah?'

'She tried to take the knife away from me. It was her fault.'

'Oh no it wasn't. It was your fault entirely. I really don't know what's got into you. Why do you have to behave so badly?' Bella stared at her mother and said nothing. 'Come on. Answer me.' Her voice took on a gentler approach.

'You don't care about me,' she said in a soft voice.

'Don't be silly. Of course I care for

you. Very much.' She reached out to the child and tried to hug her.

'You're always too busy for me.'

'You must understand that I have an important job to do. Now your daddy is gone from us, it's all down to me. I'm in charge of the factory and all the people who work there.'

'Paula doesn't like me very much. I'm always, always being left with her.'

'Yes, well that's because she is usually here.'

'Well you aren't here. It's like having too much school. I hate school and I don't like spending all my time with Paula. Sarah sometimes puts me to bed as well. I don't like that either.'

'Oh dear. You're in quite a mess, aren't you?'

'Yes. What are you going to do about it?'

'I'll give it some thought. I'll put you to bed now and then I'll see what we can do about the future. Come on. Go and change into your nightie. And brush your teeth.'

To her great relief, Bella did as she was told. When she was in bed, Nellie sat beside her telling her stories about her own childhood. Soon she was falling asleep and Nellie got up quietly and left her. It was something she needed to deal with, somehow. But how that was to be done, she had no idea.

In their apartment, Paula and William had been talking about the afternoon. It had been good to see his aunts and uncles.

'Your mother enjoyed herself, don't you think?' Paula said.

'I think so. But she does seem a bit stressed at the moment. Bella was dreadful, wasn't she? I can't think why she didn't come down and join us.'

'Typical Bella. Something has to be done about the child. I have a meeting after school next week so I won't be able to bring her home. I must remember to tell your mother tomorrow.'

'I'm going to finish off my letter. I need to post it tomorrow.'

'What, the job?'

'Yes. I mean to apply for it. It really does seem like the perfect opportunity.'

'I'm not sure about it, love. Doesn't it seem a bit . . . well, disloyal? I mean, you'll be leaving your mother in the lurch, won't you?'

'She won't let me take on anything else. I'll leave everything set up for the coronation stuff. They can finish it off without me and if they don't get any more orders, well so be it. Mother doesn't seem to think it's worth it anyway. She wants everyone to carry on with the same old stuff. No, I really think it's time for me to move on.'

'Whatever you think is right. But we will have to find somewhere else to live. Seems a shame after we've got this place so nice.'

'Thanks, Paula. It means a lot that you are supportive. If we do have to move, I promise we'll find somewhere just as nice, if not even nicer.'

8

Nellie decided to get someone to come and look after Bella. If she met her from school and stayed with her until she came home herself, it should make things easier for Paula. She went to speak to Paula about her plans.

'So if you can bring her home for this week, I'll try to organise something as soon as possible.'

'I'm afraid I have two meetings after school this week, but I'll bring her home the other days. It would be good if someone was here for her. I think it might help quite a lot.'

'Oh dear, that's not very convenient.' Nellie sounded rather irritated and Paula felt it was necessary to apologise. 'Can't be helped I suppose. I'll see if Sarah can do it on those days. Very well.' She left her daughter-in-law standing by her door.

'I'm sorry,' Paula called after her

retreating figure, but Nellie hadn't seemed to notice. She gave a shrug and went back inside. 'Your mother isn't pleased with me,' she called out to her husband.

William posted his letter on his way to work and felt very anxious about the possibility of getting an interview. He did his work as normal and avoided seeing his mother whenever possible. She seemed to be very involved in meetings and left him to his own devices. He did not feel very happy about what he was doing and wanted more responsibility. Hopefully that would come if he was interviewed.

'I've got an interview for Bella. She's going to be assessed on Thursday. I'm so pleased about it.' Paula was full of her news when William came in.

'Good. It should help at least to have a diagnosis. I posted my letter and now it's a case of waiting.'

'I thought I'd make something nice for supper. I got some fish and thought I'd make a fish pie. How does that sound to you?'

'Fine. Whatever you like. How long do you think it will be before I hear?'

'How do I know? I've no idea how long these things take.'

'I hope it doesn't take too long. I can't stand the waiting.'

'Try to occupy your mind with something else then. Think about what you'll do if you don't get an interview.'

'I suppose I'll just be plodding on with more of the same. Maybe I'll go and look at the shops in town. Eye up the competition. See what other people are doing. Yes, I'll do that tomorrow.'

'Good. You could always peel some potatoes for now, if you want to help.'

'Peel potatoes? Oh. I suppose I could.'

'The knife's in the drawer and the potatoes are in the vegetable rack. I should think three of them will do.'

'Yes, ma'am. Whatever you say.'

Paula smiled as her husband picked up three potatoes and proceeded to peel them.

'I think maybe you might need to do

another one,' she laughed. He'd taken off a great deal of potato with his peel. She prepared the fish and put it into a pan with some milk. They worked together quietly and soon she was ready to mash the potatoes. 'There,' she said when the pie was assembled. 'It can go into the oven now. Half an hour and we can eat.'

'Let's have something to drink. There's some sherry left over from Christmas. I want to celebrate.'

'I'm not sure what you want to celebrate.'

'I feel optimistic about this new job. Isn't that a good enough reason?' He went to the sideboard and took out the remains of the Christmas sherry. He poured a glass for each of them and raised his in a toast. 'Here's to the future,' he said. Paula drank with him.

'Whatever the future might bring.'

'How was Bella today?'

'Same as usual. She came back here with me for a while and then went down to the kitchen. I assume that's where she went, anyway.'

'Does she know about the test?'

'Not yet. I need to tell Nellie and see if she's willing to come along. Do you think she might?'

'I doubt it somehow. She's so involved with taking over everything. She doesn't want my father to be missed.'

'It's such a shame really.' They talked on for a while until Paula looked at the time. 'I'll see how the pie's getting on. We may be able to eat soon.'

Later that evening, Paula decided to go and talk to Nellie about her daughter. She was working in the breakfast room, favouring it more than the dining room now she was eating alone.

'Excuse me interrupting you, but I needed to have a word about Bella.'

'Oh no. What has she done now?'

'Nothing. It's about the test. Dyslexia? You remember I said I wanted to put her in for it? Well, they are coming on Thursday at eleven o'clock. I wondered if you could be there?'

'Thursday? I'm sorry but I have meetings on Thursday. I could do Friday afternoon.'

'I'm sorry but they are coming on Thursday. We don't have a choice in the system. They come when they say they're coming.'

'That's not very convenient for you, is it, dear? Nor for me, actually.'

'And you can't put off your meeting, I suppose?'

'Not really.'

'Couldn't William help with it?'

'William? Oh no. It's a senior management issue.'

Paula bit her lip. It seemed to her that Nellie was just being difficult. Of course William could do it, but Nellie's resistance to her son's abilities was more noticeable than ever.

'Very well. If you can't be there for Bella, then that's that. I'll try to be around for her but I do have my class to manage. Sorry to have bothered you.' She left feeling rather annoyed. She could never imagine her own mother putting any sort of meeting before seeing to her daughter's welfare. But then, her mother was nothing like Nellie.

In the breakfast room, Nellie sighed. She knew she had handled it all rather badly. She was running interviews for a child minder later in the week. She glanced at her diary. That was on Thursday, too, but not until the evening. Could she miss out on the management meeting? William would be there anyway, so maybe he could chair it. No, it certainly wouldn't do to leave him in charge of anything so big. Once she had her second-in-command, everything would be so much easier. Bella would have to manage on her own.

She carried on reading her reports. She paused again. The child had behaved herself since Sunday, hadn't she? Nobody had complained about her, so Nellie assumed all was well. She'd been to see her in bed, hadn't she? The fact that she was asleep hadn't really mattered to her, but she made a note to mention it to the child the next day. She needed to know she was loved.

Nellie left her work for the rest of the evening and gave thought to her daughter. She was such a pretty little thing. Remembering her behaviour from Sunday, she frowned. Was it simply her trying to get extra attention? Or was there really something wrong with her? She gave it some serious thought. Paula should really know the child. She was a teacher after all, and usually very patient. Perhaps she should go and talk more to her daughter-in-law. It was only nine o'clock. She went upstairs to the apartment and knocked at the door.

'Paula dear, I wonder if we could talk a little?'

'Of course. Come in. Excuse the mess; I'm just sorting out some stuff for school tomorrow.'

'I wanted to talk to you about Bella.'

'Oh, yes?'

'I've been putting her out of my mind recently. I hadn't realised the problems you've been having with the child. When I saw her on Sunday, I realised I've been ignoring what you were telling me. Oh hello, William. I was just having a talk to Paula.' William had appeared in the sitting room.

'Do you want me to go away?'

'No, it's fine. So what exactly are these tests she's going to have?'

'Mostly to do with reading. I'm convinced she can't see the words properly, and her behaviour has gone from bad to worse. If she can't read, and writing is difficult for her, she gets bored and behaves badly. It's my theory of course. I may be wrong.'

'It all sounds feasible. And what benefit would I bring to the situation?'

'You'd be supporting Bella, mainly. Give her the encouragement she needs. Do you think you might manage it? To be at the meeting?'

'I'll see if I can change my own meeting. I do seem to be hidebound by wretched meetings at the moment. I'm trying to catch up with everything James used to do.'

'Perhaps you should aim a little lower. Not try to do everything he did, as well as the jobs you've always done. Still, what do I know about it all?' Paula felt she may have said a bit too much.

'You're possibly right. I'll let you know what happens anyway. Thanks, Paula. William.'

'Good night, Mother. Sleep well.'

She left the pair at their door and went off to her own room. It felt empty and lonely.

'Oh James,' she muttered. 'Why oh why did you have to leave me like this? It's all too much for me to handle alone.' She got herself ready for bed and settled down to what she expected would be another long night without sleep. For once she was wrong. She slept well until dawn, when she awoke feeling strangely refreshed. Never let it be said that the odd early night didn't benefit a person.

Thursday came along and Nellie arrived at the school at ten-thirty. The staff were going back to lessons after their break. The head came to speak to her.

'How nice to see you here, Mrs Cobridge. We're delighted you could manage it. I assume Mrs Cobridge, the junior one that is, has filled you in on the details of the tests?'

'A little bit.' Nellie felt intimidated by this rather superior-sounding woman. 'But I'm sure you can tell me more?'

'Not really. This is the first time we've undertaken such a test here. I know Paula had looked into it thoroughly before asking for it.'

'I see. Can I go to see her room now, then?'

'Of course. I'll show you the way.'

She was led along several corridors until she reached the door of the classroom. She knocked and opened it.

'Mummy!' called out Bella. 'What are you doing here? I haven't been naughty, I promise.'

'I'm sure you haven't. I came to see how you're getting on.' She was flannelling, assuming the child knew what was going to happen.

'Your mummy's here because there's

someone going to come and listen to you reading. She wants to hear how you get on.'

'That's silly. Everyone knows I can't read.'

'Perhaps you'd like to take Bella and go along to the room we're going to be using?' Paula said, desperate to get some order back into the rest of class. They were hanging onto every word being spoken and some of them were talking to their friends, asking if Bella was about to be expelled. 'Come on then everyone, you have work to do. Settle down please.'

Nellie walked along the corridor holding her daughter's little hand firmly in her own. The head was leading the way and opened a small door off to one side of the corridor.

'You can wait in here. The dyslexia specialist will be arriving soon.'

'Thank you,' Nellie said politely. 'Come and sit beside me, Bella.' After a few minutes, the door opened and a young woman came in.

'Hello. I'm Maisie Greenwood. And you must be Bella?' she said kindly.

'I'm Nellie Cobridge. Bella's mother.'

'Pleased to meet you. Now this isn't going to be too difficult, Bella. I want to see how well you can read.'

'Can't read at all,' she replied, hiding behind her mother's skirt.

'Then let's see exactly what we can do to help you, shall we?'

The young woman was behaving in a very grown-up manner, thought Nellie. She responded to all of Bella's complaints in a workmanlike way and soon the little girl was reading some words. Nellie sat quietly and listened to her tests, feeling very pleased she had made the decision to come and be with her daughter.

It was an hour later when Maisie finally said, 'Thank you very much, Bella. You've done very well. I want to speak to your mother now and then to your teacher. You'll soon be reading as well as the rest of your class, providing you follow my instructions. And no more silly behaviour, do you understand?'

'Yes, miss. Have I got to go back to my class now?'

'Yes. You go along. I should think it's almost lunch time, isn't it?'

'I 'spect so. It'll be horrible anyway. It always is.'

'And what did I say about behaving properly?'

'Yes, miss. Bye. See you tonight, Mummy.'

'Of course you will, dear. Enjoy the rest of the day.'

The two adults watched as she left them. Then Maisie spoke to her mother.

'She has very severe dyslexia. There are various ways we can treat it. I'll speak to Mrs Cobridge during her lunch break. It would certainly help to have a specialist coming into school for at least one lesson a week. I'm not sure about whether you can pay for that?'

'Of course. I'll pay whatever you need me to pay.'

'That's helpful.'

'Do you need me to pay you?'

'Oh no. I'm part of the school's services.'

'You're very young for such a responsible job,' Nellie told her. She smiled. 'Sorry. I shouldn't have said that.'

'No worries. I do have a degree in the subject though. One of the first in the country. Or should I say females in the country. I'm delighted to have got the job.'

'I'm sure you're very well qualified.'

'It's practice really. I am actually dyslexic.'

'Goodness. I could never tell. How do you manage?'

'I have overcome some of the difficulties.'

'And you've got a degree?'

'I had help. I want you to realise Bella can have similar help. It really shouldn't impair her chances for a good education.'

'Well, you've really opened my eyes. Thank you very much for taking such time and trouble with my daughter. I'll certainly be glad to give her whatever help she might need.'

'There's nothing better than your time. Goodbye now. Thank you for coming along today.'

'Goodbye. Keep in touch.'

Nellie left the little room and felt very pleased she had made the effort to attend. What had the girl said? *There's nothing better than your time.* That was going to be difficult but it was something she must try to do. Perhaps she could get someone who knew about dyslexia to come and look after the little girl. She mustn't rely on her maid or cook to look after her daughter. She now had a diagnosis and needed to get someone professional in to help. Perhaps Paula would be able to help her find the right person. She glanced at her wristwatch and hurried back to work.

Nellie got home relatively early for her. She found Bella in the kitchen and took her up to the breakfast room.

'I thought we'd have tea together today,' she said.

'I've had my tea. I got some when I came in. Cook always gives me some tea.'

'Oh I see. Then shall we do some reading together?'

'I don't want to. I've done reading all day long. I want to play something. Will you play a game with me?'

'All right. What would you like to play?'

'Cowboys. You can be the Indian and I catch you and tie you up. Then I kill you.'

'Bella, really. I don't know where you get such peculiar ideas. I was thinking of Ludo or something similar.'

'Ludo? Whatever's that?'

'I'm sure there's a set in the nursery. Let's go and look.' Could her child have reached seven years of age and she didn't know what the game of Ludo was? They went into the nursery. It smelt stale and unloved. She opened the cupboard and found the old Ludo set. The box was pretty battered but it seemed as if the counters were all there and the dice as well. 'Good, it's all here. Let's take it down.'

Bella seemed interested and Nellie wanted to capitalise on it. Perhaps it wasn't too late to begin to form a proper relationship with the child. She explained the rules and they began to play. As it was purely a game of chance, she couldn't let the child win, and soon she was in a commanding position.

'I've only got to get my next counter round to home and I've won.'

'Stupid game,' announced Bella. 'Don't like it.'

'Go on. Throw the dice again. There. See? You've sent me right back to the start.'

'Why?'

'Because you landed on top of me.'

'Like cowboys and Indians?'

'Not really. But now you have the chance of winning.'

Everything changed from that moment on. Bella saw the whole game as a competition and when she finally managed to win, she was jubilant.

'I won, I won! I beat Mummy! Brilliant game.' She ran round the room screeching until Nellie told her it was bedtime.

'Go on now, dear. We'll play again soon. Go and have a wash and brush your teeth. I'll come and put you to bed.'

'Will you tell me some more stories about when you were a little girl?'

'All right. If you go to bed now and don't take too long.'

It seemed this was the way to get round her daughter. The girl this morning had said that her time was the most important thing. Somehow, she had to make sure she had some time to give her daughter.

'See, James? I am beginning to manage without you.' She wiped away a tear and went to Bella's room to see her into bed.

9

Paula saw William's letter when she came home that evening. She hoped he wouldn't be late home from work, as it might say if he had an interview with Jerome and Company. She fingered the envelope and wondered what it said. She heard Nellie arrive home and hoped her husband wouldn't be too far behind her. At last he came in and looked exhausted.

'There's a letter for you. From Jerome's.'

'Oh my goodness, that was quick. They mustn't want me if it's that quick.' He ripped it open and read it. 'Yes!' he called out. 'They want to interview me on Monday next. They say I've got a good chance.'

'Congratulations, darling. I'm so pleased for you. What do they say?'

'*Thank you for your application. We*

159

are pleased to ask you to come in on Monday next for an interview. You have excellent qualifications for the job we are seeking to fill and we wish you every success. Then a lot of stuff about going to their office and other formalities. The good thing is, I have excellent qualifications. Oh Paula, this is splendid news. Even if I don't get the job, wherever it is, it means I can look elsewhere. I'm not tied to Cobridge's factory any more. Well, not without some responsibility at least.' There was a knock at their door. 'It must be Mother, or someone from the house. I'll put this letter away, and don't mention it.'

'I'll answer the door. You ready?' He nodded.

'Hallo, dear. Can I come in? I don't want to interrupt your meal or anything.'

'I'm rather late. I haven't got it ready yet. Please come in. Did you want to see William?'

'No, it's you I needed to see.'

'Oh, about Bella? I met with Maisie after your session. Was she useful to you?'

'She's certainly made me think a lot. I was wondering if you know of anyone I could employ to help her? I was going to get someone to look after her after school and I thought if it was someone who might be able to help with the dyslexia too, it might help her.'

'It's quite an idea. I can't think of anyone offhand, but I'll ask around at school. I'm afraid it's rather a specialist subject really. We're going to have someone coming into school twice a week to help Bella, but someone here every day? I think that's pretty optimistic.'

'I see. Well, it was worth my while asking. If you do find anyone, let me know. If not, I'll go to the agency place again. They usually come up with someone to do what I ask. Mind you, since the last war, not everyone wants to work at household chores. I suppose we're lucky to still have Cook and Sarah.'

'I suppose you are really. Cook's been

with you a good many years now. Hopefully she'll stay till she retires.'

'What on earth will I do then?' said Nellie sadly. 'I'd better go now and let you get your supper.'

'You could stay if you'd like to,' offered Paula.

'I won't thank you. Bit late to let cook know. She'll have prepared something for me, I expect. Enjoy your evening. Bye, my dears.'

'Good night.' Paula shut the door behind her.

'Why on earth did you invite her to stay? She might have said yes, and then where would we have been?'

Paula giggled. 'You'd have been polite and not mentioned the subject that's burning holes in you. Go on, read your letter again. Tell me about it all over again.' He did. Several times that evening.

It seemed a long time until Monday. They spent Sunday lunchtime with Nellie and Bella. The latter seemed a little better behaved and William commented on it.

'You seem happier, little Bella.'

'Mummy's been home in time to play Ludo with me twice. I like Ludo. I could teach you how to play it if you like.'

'Perhaps we could all have a game after lunch,' suggested Nellie.

'All right, we will. You won't mind, will you, Paula?'

'Not at all. But I should warn you, I'm quite a demon at that game. You'll have to watch out.' Bella squealed with joy and clapped her hands together.

'This is good. I'll beat all of you. When can we start?'

'When lunch is all eaten and cleared away.'

Bella scoffed the rest of her plateful right away and sat waiting for everyone else to catch up. 'Come on,' she told them. 'Hurry up.' At last they were all finished and went through into the drawing room. 'I'll set the table out,' the child said, collecting the card table from the corner. It hadn't been used in several months and the moths had got into it. 'It doesn't matter,' Bella said. 'The board will cover up the holes.'

They played several games, with Bella squealing excitedly when she was winning. The adults drank their coffee between shakes of the dice and did actually quite enjoy themselves. At last Nellie called for a truce.

'I'm sure William and Paula have other things to do this afternoon, or what's left of it.'

'Yes, indeed,' agreed Paula. 'I'm sure William has things he needs to do as well.' She smiled at him knowingly.

'I'll be out of the factory tomorrow. I'm, er, going to do a bit of a looking round some of the shops. See what everyone else is doing. For the coronation, of course.'

'Only three months left now,' said Nellie.

'Oh, did I say, I've got one of the local companies interested in buying a whole lot of the little mugs? They want to give every child in their county one as a souvenir.'

'No, you hadn't told me. Congratulations. That'll be quite a sizeable order.'

'Several thousand pounds. And there may be more. I've sent samples out all over the place.' Nellie stared at him.

'Really? Will you be able to fill the orders if you get them?'

'Oh yes. Providing I have the staff, of course.'

'I am surprised. Well done, then.'

'Thank you, Mother.' He paused, wondering whether to say anything more. 'Shall we go back to the apartment, Paula?' She nodded and thanked her mother-in-law politely for lunch. Back upstairs, she laughed.

'I really thought you were going to say something to her about this interview.'

'Course not. I wanted to leave her thinking I'm not completely useless though.'

'You've done very well with your mugs. Let's hope some other places also buy them and you make a fortune for the company. Before you leave I mean, of course.'

'Always assuming I get this other job. If I don't, well at least I'm doing pretty well with my special lines. Oh dear. I wish tomorrow was over.'

'You'll be fine. Just you wait and see.'

★　★　★

'William Cobridge,' he said, holding out his hand to the gentleman behind the desk.

'How do you do. Cobridge. That's an interesting name.'

'Well yes. I'm James Cobridge's son.' The man stared at him but said nothing.

'I see. Well, Mr Cobridge, tell me about your work and what you hope to achieve by applying for this job.'

'I've worked in my father's factory for several years. He died a few weeks ago and since then, well my mother has taken over much of the responsibility for everything. Just about everything anyway. I have asked for more responsibility but she is unwilling to share it. I saw this job advertised and decided to apply for it. It seems to encompass just about everything I've been looking for.' Once he had begun, he continued in the same vein, telling Mr Jerome all about his plans for the future how he saw the business developing after the coronation.

'It seems to me you have a fair bit of responsibility already,' he commented.

'Well yes. But it's in a very limited way.'

Mr Jerome was smiling. Why was he smiling? William felt annoyed but he knew better than to show it. They talked for some time, him asking questions and his candidate answering them.

'Is there anything else you'd like to tell me? Or indeed, to ask me?'

'What are my chances? I mean, will you be recommending me for a further interview?'

'Oh I should think so. There are one or two other candidates I still have to see.'

'And when will I hear?'

'I'll speak to our client before the weekend. Thank you very much for coming along today. It has been interesting and a pleasure to have met you.'

'Thank you, Mr Jerome. And thank you for the time.'

'Not at all. Goodbye, Mr Cobridge.'

'Goodbye, sir.' He went out of the office, wondering how on earth he'd got on. Why was the man so amused? He shook his head and decided to go to the shops for his look around. It was only half-past eleven.

Back in his office, Mr Jerome came to a decision. He lifted the phone and asked to speak to Nellie.

Towards the end of the day, Nellie called William into her office.

'I had a call from Mr Jerome this morning,' she said. William blushed.

'Really?' he stammered.

'He had just interviewed someone for the job. He seemed quite impressed with the candidate.'

William sat silently for a few minutes and then drew in his breath. 'You mean it was here? You advertised for an assistant manager?'

'Yes. So, why did you apply for it?'

'I didn't know it was for here. He managed to keep very quiet about that. I did ask him where the job was, but he wouldn't tell me. I'm sorry if you thought I was being disloyal, but you must understand why I did it.'

'I think so. He said you wanted more responsibility. To take on more things.'

'I think I'm ready for it. I know you don't want to relinquish anything yet, but it's important for the company. If we're going to grow, then we must implement new ideas. You seem to want to stay in the past glories. But we do need to move forward.'

'I see. You'd better give me your ideas in a report. Tell me how you see the company going in the next few years.'

He stared at his mother. Where was the simple girl who had married into this family? She seemed to have changed completely. Ever since his father had died, she'd changed. He wasn't really sure he was completely happy with it, but it was a fact and he needed to address it.

'I'll make a start right away. I'll have it with you by tomorrow.'

'Thank you.'

'Does this mean you're considering me for the job?'

'We'll have to wait and see.'

He stared at her once again. Then he rose and left her office, never looking back. He'd be dammed if he was going to lose his chance. He wanted this job more than he had ever wanted anything in his life. He was going to work for it and make her see that he was the only person who was really right for it. Would he go home now and work on his report through the evening, or would he stay and work on it here? It was already nearly home time. He went back to his tiny office and packed up his briefcase. He picked up a few documents and carried them with him. He would go home now and spend his evening working. He knew Paula would support him. Besides, he needed to tell her his latest news. She didn't even know the result of his interview.

'You're home early,' Paula said when he walked in. 'How did it go?'

'You're never going to believe me. It was Cobridge's that asked them to do the interviews. Can you believe it? My mother had organised a company to do interviews and then make a shortlist. Thinking about it, I'm really shocked. She didn't even consider me a suitable person to do this poxy job.'

'Maybe you're just too close.'

'I'm absolutely furious, the more I think about it.'

'I hope you haven't told her.'

'Course not. She wants me to do a report showing the changes I might bring in. How I see the future. I seriously think she's gone power-mad. I think she's getting out of her depth. You don't remember the woman who married my father. She was quite shy

171

and when she had to take over running this house, she found it quite a burden. She'd been a maid and now she was mistress. Before I was born of course.'

'Perhaps you need to calm down a bit. Do the report and see how you feel after that. I'll put the dinner on while you think about what you need to write.'

'I suppose so. You're right. I need to make it good and sound authoritative. Thanks, love. I knew you'd support me.'

'Give me something worth supporting then.'

He worked solidly for most of the evening. He produced a huge pile of papers and then sat back. 'I really ought to get this typed. It looks pretty amateurish, being hand-written. Trouble is, I don't have anyone who could do it for me. Well, nobody I could trust.'

'I could do it. If we had a typewriter at home, of course.'

'I suppose we could go into the office and do it.'

'What, now?'

'Or early in the morning.'

'I'd rather go now and get it done. It's only half-past nine. We could be back by midnight.'

'If you're sure. Okay, let's do it. Thank you, darling. It's very good of you.'

'All part of the war effort. I want to see you getting on. I may not be able to make much progress at school, but at least I can support you. I'll get my coat.'

They crept out of the house, not wanting to alert Nellie to their plans. William drove to the factory and took out his keys.

'There'll be a night shift but we can get in through the door at the bottom. Come on.' He held Paula's hand as they went inside. He spoke to the night watchman and said he was going up to the office.

He unlocked the door and showed Paula the typewriter. 'Can you manage this one?'

'I think so. I had to learn at school.

I'm not all that quick though. I want to get it right first time.'

'You'll be fine. Thank you so much.'

She worked through the various pages of his report. When she reached the end, she said, 'I hope that's all right? I must say, it's very good. I was most impressed with what you've written. I hope your mother is too.'

'She'd damned well better be. Come on then. Let's get home and get you to bed. You'll be very tired tomorrow.'

They were both awake early the next day. William was excited at the prospect of showing his mother the report and Paula felt excited on his behalf. She went off to school, wishing she could be a fly on the wall in Nellie's office. *Woe betide any children who get on the wrong side of me today* were her main thoughts.

William took his report to Nellie and handed it over to her. She put it to one side and thanked him.

'Aren't you going to read it?' he demanded.

'Later, dear. I have some other things to look at first.'

'We stayed up half the night to get it ready for you. Paula typed it too.'

'I didn't realise she could type. I'll look at it later today.'

'Mother,' he exclaimed. 'I hope you realise what this means to us. I can't believe you're putting something else as being more important to you. If this is your attitude, perhaps I was being sensible in looking for another job. I didn't know I was applying to be your assistant, but gave it my best shot. I want to improve my circumstances. I'm sure Father would have made me your assistant manager. He trusted me. Look how much money I've made on the coronation stuff.' He ran out of steam and paused.

'Very well. I'll look at your report right away. Go away and leave me the space to read it.' She picked up the report and began to read it.

'I'll be next door,' he promised.

Nellie read through his ideas. She

smiled. How like his father he was. Even the phrases he used. She had to admit, he had expressed some good ideas, and Mr Jerome had been right — he was a natural for the job. If this was typical of his plans, they would be well set up for the coming months. She had herself thought of some of his ideas but hadn't worked out how to accomplish them. Her expertise was in decoration and following that side of things through. Perhaps it was indeed time to relinquish some of her powers to her son. It would mean more time for her to spend with her daughter and socialising a little. She opened some of the envelopes on her desk and attended to one or two other matters. Then she picked up her phone and dialled William's number.

'Would you come into the office, please.'

Seconds later, he was there. 'Well? What do you think?'

'I've read your report. I think you have some good ideas. Very well, I shall appoint you as my assistant manager. We'll discuss the terms of the job and I'll instruct accounts to pay you an increase in salary right away. Now, go and sort out your coronation stuff. I'll meet with you again later today.'

'Thank you, Mother. I promise you're not going to be disappointed. I really will work very hard and make you proud of me.'

'You'd best not let me down, son. I dunna think you will or I'd not be trustin' ya with the task.' She was laughing as she spoke in the Potteries dialect.

'I wunna do that, Mum. I'll mek ya proud on me.' He laughed as well, copying her accent.

He danced along the corridor and swung round the top of the stairs, leaping down them three at a time. How soon could he make his new role known? He would wait for his mother to announce it. That way it would make a proper impact. He assumed she'd tell Mr Jerome to cancel any further interviews. Oh, and he would definitely need a proper office. He looked into several of the rooms, as if trying to decide which one he'd choose. It was only Tuesday but he felt as if he'd worked a full week. He would take Paula out for a slap-up meal. He lifted the telephone and dialled Paula's school.

'May I speak to Mrs Cobridge please? It's important. Yes, I know she'll be in her classroom. Yes, please. It won't take long.'

'Hallo?' said Paula's voice, sounding a little strained.

'You are speaking to the new assistant manager of Cobridge's,' he announced. He heard her catch her breath.

'Very good. Oh yes, I am pleased. Thank you for letting me know.'

'We're going out for dinner tonight. To celebrate.'

'Very well. Thank you again. Bye.'

'Bye,' he said to the phonepiece in his hand. 'She didn't seem overly excited.' Then he realised she'd been in the head's study and couldn't show any excitement. Ah well, at least she now knew. He could imagine her trying to explain the call to the head and her embarrassment. He gave a shrug and went to check on his workers. They really did feel like *his* workers now. He looked at the heaps of beautiful plates, all with gold edges and the badge in the middle. They were selling very well. People were buying them for their families, a memento of the events that were being planned in London. He moved on to the little mugs, again with gilded handles and the official coronation badges on them. He needed to get samples sent to other county towns to make sure they saw what Cobridge china could offer. He made a call to his sales team.

'I want us to have a meeting later today. Everyone who is around is to attend. We have goods to sell, gentlemen.' He felt empowered and ready to do battle.

10

Things had been rather quiet during the day. William felt disappointed that no announcement had been made. At the end of the day he was ready to leave, when one of the workers came to him and congratulated him.

'Thank you. But how did you hear?'

'Factory's buzzin' wi' it. Missus Nellie put up a sign. Someone read it us and it seems you're now deputy boss. So congratu . . . whatsists.'

He scurried off and William was left standing there. He felt a sense of relief. Until others knew, he'd wondered if his mother was going to back down and make it an unofficial appointment. He decided to go to his mother's office and thank her again for having confidence in him.

'Ah, William. You've no doubt heard that I put up a notice. We shall need to organise an office for you. And some secretarial help. Can't have you go taking stuff home for Paula to type.'

'Well thanks, Mother. I was wondering when you'd announce it. I thought I'd take Paula out tonight as a sort of celebration.'

'Good idea. I was wondering if I might accompany you? It's certainly time I was going out again. I can't believe it's nearly two months since James passed on. Oh dear, I suppose it is all right for me to be seen out again?'

'I should think so. Maybe you need to dress slightly ... well, not in anything too bright.'

'You're quite right, dear. Actually, no, I won't come with you. You probably want to celebrate yourselves without this old crock with you. I'll have a quiet dinner at home.'

'You're very welcome to come. Paula won't mind.'

'It's a bit late to warn Cook. She'll have got something prepared by now.'

'As you like. So, where do you think

my new office will be?'

'You can move into mine. It looks as if I'm going to be keeping this one anyway. My secretary can do your mail too, for now. I doubt there'll be a vast amount more.'

'That sounds fine. She's already been doing most of it anyway. Thanks again for trusting me, Mother.'

'Come here, lad.' He got up and went to her. She gave him a big hug and held on to him for quite a while. He felt her shake slightly and moved away. Her eyes were damp and she looked very sad.

'What is it?' he asked.

'Nothin' really. I miss your dad summat chronic. It just reminded me, givin' you a hug like that. I can't even remember the last time we had a hug.'

'Nor can I. We should do it more often.'

'Mebbe. Mebbe. Now, get yourself home. You've got a wife waiting for you.'

'Night, Mother. Mum,' he added.

'Geroff, ya cheeky sod,' he heard as he left her. He almost ran along the corridor for the second time that day.

The young pair dined at a smart restaurant in Stoke. William had ordered champagne and by the end of the meal, they were both slightly squiffy.

'Coffee, sir?' the waiter asked tactfully.

'Certainly do. Need to sober up before I drive us home.' He giggled slightly and hiccupped.

'Are you all right, darling?' asked Paula.

'Course I am. Assistant manager at Cobridge's — how could I not be? I feel very good. Very, very good.'

His wife laughed softly. 'I know you do, but can you actually drive us home?'

'Not sure. But you can.'

Paula had been having lessons for some while and was waiting for her driving test to come through. She wasn't sure it was a good idea as she had also drunk some champagne. Not as much as William by any means, but she wasn't a confident driver at all.

'Let's have some coffee and see after that,' she said. 'We could always get a taxi and come back tomorrow to fetch the car.'

They each drank two cups of coffee and William considered he was now quite sober enough to drive the few miles home. 'I'll be extra careful,' he promised. 'Drive slowly and all that.'

It was not a comfortable drive home at all. He drove at twenty miles an hour on average and when they finally turned into the drive at Cobridge House, Paula was quite shaken.

'See? I did it. Quite safely.'

'Apart from practically terrifying me half to death and jumping a set of traffic lights.'

'But nobody saw me. That's what's important. Nobody saw me at all.'

'Except me. I saw everything. I really wish I had driven. But it was a lovely evening and I'm very proud of you. Come on now, let's go inside.'

'Perfect end to a perfect day,' he said, slightly drunkenly.

'Nice evening?' asked Nellie as they went across the hall. She was standing at one side and watched them as William staggered along to the stairs.

'Wonderful, thank you, Mum.'

Paula stared at his use of the term of address. Mum? Where did that come from? He always called her 'Mother'.

'Very nice, thank you, Nellie,' Paula said. 'Now I need to get this man off to bed. Have you had a nice evening?' she asked politely.

'Usual. You're right though. You need to get him to bed. I hope he didn't drive home in that state.'

'Oh no. I drove us back,' she lied.

'Well done, dear. I hope this was a one-occasion lapse. Good night.'

The two of them went upstairs to the apartment, both of them giggling like a pair of school children.

'What did you say? You had driven back? You liar. I shall have to tickle you into submission.'

'No, don't you dare. No, William. Stop it.'

They both regretted having to get up so early the following day. They both felt rather bleary-eyed and went off to work slightly the worse for wear. It seemed a long day for Paula, with Bella returning to her poor behaviour. She actually went to the head to ask if she had heard anything from the dyslexia people. There was no news.

'Can't we ring them to ask what's happening?' Paula asked in some desperation.

'I'm sorry but it really isn't done. We'll just have to wait to see what they come up with.'

'I just hope I can keep her in my classroom. She is a nightmare. Being related to her makes matters so much worse.'

'Very well. I suggested you send her along to me for a lesson. I can have her here in my room with her work. At least it will give you a chance to teach the rest of the class and me an opportunity to see what she's like.'

'Thank you very much. It would

certainly be a help next lesson in particular. I'll sort out something she should be able to do and bring her along after break.' The head nodded her assent and Paula went to her room to sort out some material for the child. She took it along to the head's room and left it on the small desk to one side. The head had disappeared. When the bell rang she took her class to her room and set them to work.

'Now Bella, I want you to come with me. You're going to do some work in the head's room. The rest of you, carry on with the work and no noise. Do you understand me?'

Murmuring of 'Yes, miss' reached her ears and she left them. Holding Bella's hand firmly, she led her to the head's room. She was still away. Now what should she do? She couldn't leave the child on her own. Goodness knew what she would have got up to.

'It looks as if she's forgotten,' Paula muttered angrily. 'You'd better come back with me.' Bella danced along beside her, skipping and bouncing up and down.

'She doesn't want me, does she?'

'I think she's just rather busy. Stop bouncing and come along quietly.' She continued to bounce along the corridor. Paula decided to ignore her and went back to her room.

'I thought Bella wasn't coming back, miss,' said one of the children.

'The head is busy at the moment. Bella is coming back and is going to behave beautifully, aren't you, Bella?'

'No.'

'You are.'

'No, I'm not.'

Paula ignored the child and began her lesson. She was teaching about the Romans and how they influenced our lives today. Bella was wandering round poking the other children and generally being a nuisance. Suddenly Paula lost her temper. She had had enough of the child and her behaviour.

'You are a very naughty little girl. I'm sick of you always interrupting what I am trying to do and making noises.' Bella stood silently, amazed at the tone of her teacher's voice. 'You stop the others from making progress and upset them all the time. Unless you can sit quietly, you can get out of my class. I've had enough. Do you hear me?'

Bella stared back at her and eventually went to her seat and sat down. She was shocked. Nobody had ever spoken to her with so much anger and she didn't quite know how to take it. Paula took a deep breath and continued to teach the rest of the class. Bella actually did try to work quite well and at the end of the lesson she hung back, waiting for Paula to say something to her.

'Go along to lunch now.'

'Was I good for the rest of the lesson?' she asked somewhat more quietly.

'Quite good. But you need to behave like that all the time. Now go and get your lunch.' Bella left the classroom and disappeared along towards the dining hall. Paula gave a sigh and went to the staffroom. She took out her sandwiches and sat eating them silently. The head came in.

'Oh Paula, I'm so sorry. I was called away and it took almost all of the lesson. How was she?'

'I'm afraid I lost my temper with her and shouted at her. She sat down and worked for the rest of the lesson. Not up to the rest of the class's standard, but at least she tried. I feel rather ashamed.'

'Not at all. It's probably exactly what she needed. Do you want me to have her this afternoon?'

'I'll give her a try with the rest of the group. They'll be painting and she does actually quite like that.'

'Very well. I should be in my office if you do need me.'

'Thank you very much.' She left Paula on her own and she thought what a lovely person her head teacher was. She was very understanding and helpful, clearly a good teacher. It was a pity when a really good teacher became a headmistress, as they no longer actually did much teaching. Still, it meant she was more understanding towards the teachers who were having problems.

When Paula had finished her lunch, she decided to go for a walk outside. It was a nice day and she felt like getting some air. She left the school building and went along the street a little way, deciding to walk to the park. She speeded her pace, knowing she'd have to be quick if she was to be back in time. She would go in at one gate and out at another further along the road. She saw someone ahead of her and as she came closer, she saw it was Bella.

'Bella,' she called out. 'What on earth are you doing here? You know you shouldn't leave the school building.'

'Nobody wants me there. So I decided to leave. I'm going home now.'

'You are not. You're coming back with me.' She took hold of her hand and led her unwillingly back to school.

'You will go and sit in the head's room this afternoon. She will make sure you do some work too.' Paula felt very angry again, and also extremely worried that the child had left school so easily. 'Have you had some lunch?' she asked suddenly, realising she must have left school some time ago.

'No. Didn't want any.'

'I'll see if there's anything left for you.' She took her into the dining hall, where the ladies were eating their own food. 'I'm sorry, but this one missed her lunch. Is there anything she can have?'

'Oh dear. We've just cleared everything out and washed up the tins.'

'Oh well, never mind. It's her own silly fault.'

'I could maybe make her a sandwich. There's some jam.'

'That's kind of you. Thank you very much. Bella?' She prodded the child.

'Thank you,' she responded automatically.

The lady went into the kitchen and came back with a sandwich on a plate.

'Sit down there and eat it,' Paula commanded. She stood over her until it was all gone. 'Right. Say thank you to the kind lady, and then you come with me to the head's office.'

'Thanks, miss,' she said to the lady and followed Paula out.

'What do you make of that?' said one of the ladies.

'She's a right pain, that one. Don't know how the teachers put up with her. Well you know what she's like. Tipped a whole cup of water over one of the kids last week. Should be sent somewhere, she should.'

Paula led Bella to the head's office. She told her about finding her in the park and said she'd had a sandwich. The head was quite shocked and asked Bella why she'd gone. She got the same reply as Paula.

'You can leave her here now. I'll see to her this afternoon. Enjoy your lesson.'

'Oh I will. Thank you.' She left the child and went back to her classroom, where the children were waiting in a quiet line outside. 'Very good. Come on now. I'm sorry I was late. Now, we're going to spend the afternoon doing some painting. It's a lovely day outside and I thought you could paint something nice to do with spring.' Soon they were all busily working and she went around to each of them to look at what they were doing. It was so peaceful and everyone was enjoying themselves. The difference without Bella was significant. They were a lovely group. Towards the end of the day one of the children put her hand up.

'Please, miss, can we not have Bella in our class again? It's so much better without her.'

'I know, dear, but she is a member of our group and we must try to help her.'

Several of the others put their words in and the consensus was that Bella should stay out of the group.

'I'm sorry, but she is a member of this year group. There's nothing I can do about it. Now then, clean off your brushes and the palettes. It's been a nice afternoon and I'm very pleased with all of your pictures. I think I'll make a display of them when they're all dry. Would you like that?'

'Yes, miss,' came the cry back.

When she had dismissed the children at the end of the day, she went along to the head's office.

'Bella's gone home. Someone came for her. The maid or something?'

'Oh yes. Sarah was coming today. How was she?'

'She did a little work but she certainly does have a problem with concentration. I'm not sure it's all down to the dyslexia. I'm wondering if she has some other problems too. I'm wondering if she has a degree of autism.'

'Autism? Oh goodness. We touched on that at college. I never thought of that. Have you got any literature about it? I'd like to read it and see what I think. Autism. What are the main symptoms?'

'I suppose simply put, a lack of social skills. Inability to concentrate and what appears to be generally bad behaviour. There are many angles to look at. I'll give you a book. I think there's one here. You must realise there are many aspects to it. Different levels, and not everyone is quite the same.'

'Thank you very much for this afternoon anyway. We really had a lovely time without Bella. Poor little child. Autism. I think her mother will be relieved if it does turn out to be that. I know she is worried about her daughter.'

'I thought she seemed a rather busy woman. In charge of the factory and all.'

'She is. But she does care about her daughter. I know she does.' Paula was defensive of her mother-in-law who, in honesty, she felt ignored her daughter more than she should.

'Take the book and read it and see if you agree with me. If you do, I'll get some sort of assessment done.'

'Will it mean a special school?'

'Possibly for a while at least. But there's no stigma to it. If it benefits the child, then surely it's the best solution?'

'I suppose so but I can't see Nellie — Mrs Cobridge — going along with that.'

'Perhaps she won't like it. Now, if you'll excuse me, I have things to do.'

'Sorry. Yes. I only came to say thank you for your help today. Good evening.'

'Good evening, Mrs Cobridge. See you tomorrow.'

Paula walked home, deep in thought. She felt a strange mixture of thoughts turning through her head. The book was carefully stowed in her bag and she couldn't wait to read it. She felt a mixture of apprehension at the thought of Nellie knowing there was something wrong with her daughter and elation at the thought of not having the child in her class anymore. As soon as she was home, she sat down and began to read the book. She was enthralled. By the time she had finished the third chapter, she was convinced Bella was autistic. It seemed so right in every way. She heard William coming up the stairs and gave a start. She had done nothing towards dinner. She had some chops in the fridge and quickly pushed them under the grill.

'Hallo, darling. How was your day?' She listened as he talked about the various people he'd spent time with and the jobs he'd done and overseen, all the time longing to speak about Bella and her possible diagnosis.

At last he asked, 'How was your day?'

'Interesting. Bella left school at lunchtime and went for a walk in the park. It was a miracle I found her. I'd gone there myself and spotted her. I took her back of course, and persuaded the lunchtime ladies to make her a sandwich.'

'Have you told Mother?'

'Well no. This isn't the end of it.'

'Do you mind if I go and change? I'll listen to the rest later.'

'Oh, all right then. I'll finish cooking

dinner, shall I?' He didn't reply but disappeared into the bedroom. She gave a sigh and put some carrots in to cook.

'So you see,' she continued, 'the head thinks . . . well so do I, actually. She thinks Bella is possibly autistic.'

'What will that mean for the future?'

'If she can be trained to cope with it, it shouldn't make a lot of difference to her. But it explains so much about her behaviour and her inability to learn like the other kids. I want to read some more after dinner. If you don't mind, of course.'

'You carry on. I've got some things to read too. You get on with it. I'll wash up.'

'Really? That's very good of you.'

'No problem. Go and sit down. I'll bring you some coffee too. See what an excellent husband I am?'

'I wouldn't change you for anything.' She settled down to carry on reading.

11

The next few weeks were hectic in the child's life. With Paula and the head convinced about her diagnosis, Nellie was called in to the school. The head had warned Paula not to say anything to Bella's mother until she arrived at the meeting.

'We think Bella has difficulties apart from dyslexia. We think she is autistic.'

'Autistic? What on earth is that? Is she going to die?'

'Of course not. It's a specific sort of learning difficulty. She shows all the symptoms of not being able to concentrate for long, and some anti-social tendencies. She doesn't mix with groups of people in the way most children do.'

'I see. Well yes, I agree, she does have those sorts of problems. So what do we have to do?'

'There's a special school she could attend. It does have a boarding facility. I would recommend that she should go there and see how she gets on. We'll have to get her properly assessed of course. And you could go there yourself to see it before any decisions are made.'

'How long would she have to stay there?' Nellie was beginning to feel sick. Her own little girl was being spoken about like so much meat.

'For her school days really. She would come home at holiday times, of course.'

'I don't know. It seems a bit drastic. What do you think Paula?'

Paula had been quiet until now, listening to the head talking.

'I really think it does seem like a good idea. She isn't learning much here and she does disrupt the class terribly. I'm not just saying it for my own sake. She wouldn't be in my class next term, anyway.'

'I'd like to think about it for a while. I assume we don't have to make any decisions right now?'

'Of course not,' said the head. 'I do think she will benefit though. I can give you some material to read, if you're interested.'

'Thank you, I'd like that. Boarding school, though? She's such a little girl.'

'William went to boarding school,' Paula reminded her.

'Against my better judgement. He turned into quite a snob. But he was a boy and he was older than Bella is.'

'Think about it and get back to me,' said the head. 'Now here are some leaflets, and I can loan you a book if you need it.'

Nellie rose to her feet. 'I'll look through these and ask Paula for more information if I need it.' Nellie was back in charge and swept out, wishing them a good morning.

'Do you think she'll go with the idea?' asked the head.

'I think so. She'll undoubtedly ask me loads of questions, but I think she will. I hope so. I'd better get back to my class now and relieve the supply teacher.'

'Oh, I'd wait till lunchtime now. Only another half an hour. I'm sure there's something you can do.'

'Thank you. I do have some marking.'

Over the next few days Paula expected Nellie to have some questions, but none were forthcoming. She arrived at school one morning with the announcement that she was ready for Bella to go to the new school. The head arranged for the assessment and within two weeks, she was enrolled as a pupil. Bella took to it like a duck to water and life for Paula and also the cook became peaceful once more.

★   ★   ★

It was almost June. Pretty well everything for the coronation had been taken out of the factory and was in the shops. William had done wonders with the various lines. He had sold thousands of the smallest mugs to various counties around the country, who were offering one to each child at school. The profits came from the large numbers sold. In addition to these, he had made a number of different plates, most of them similar, which could actually be sold as sets, ready for the big day itself. The factory was to be closed for the day and anyone with a television was suddenly very popular, as people all wanted to see the ceremony.

Nellie had decided to invite the family over for the occasion. Lizzie and Daniel had decided to go to his parents' to stay for a day or two, thus taking advantage of their television. This left her two brothers and their families coming to join her. Paula and William had already invited her mother and aunt to join them for the day.

'Come down and have tea with us,' Nellie invited. 'I thought we'd use some of your plates to eat from, William.'

'It's kind of you, but I thought I'd prepare something up in the apartment.

We won't want to miss any of the ceremony.'

'There'll be a pause in transmission for tea.'

'Well, if you're sure. Thank you.'

'It'll be fun to have everyone together. Lizzie and Daniel won't be with us but I'm sure we can make up for it in the rest of our family. I'll let Cook and Sarah come up to see it all too.'

'I hope you'll all get round the set. It isn't all that huge, is it?' William was slightly sceptical. 'I know we four should manage to see it all on ours.'

'There won't be so many. I did look at getting a larger set for the occasion, but nobody has one. We'll be fine with what we have. There are lots of folks don't have a set at all. Goodness, my parents would have loved all this, wouldn't they?'

'I doubt your father would. He'd have spent the day in the pub drinking himself stupid, from what you said about his past.'

'He was all right towards his end. Poor Dad. At least Mum had it a bit easier towards her end. It's the queen I feel sorry for. Lost her father and ended up having all this ceremony and stuff.'

'Yes, but she was born to it wasn't she?' Paula commented. 'It wasn't as if it was all strange to her. Mind you, she's not quite as old as I am. I wouldn't like to have to go through it all.'

'Wouldn't mind some of her jewels though,' Nellie said.

'You've got some lovely things of your own,' Paula retorted.

'You're right. I should wear some of them. I shall dress up for the big day. Make an occasion of it. I'll lend you some of them too. What would you like? Necklace and bracelet? I've got a lovely diamond set.'

'Well thank you, I'd love to. We can dress up in our best and enjoy an elegant day in diamonds.' She laughed. 'Until then, I've got a hectic day at school. The kids are so high, I don't know how to control them. We're having our own coronation tomorrow. Not sure how that's going to go.'

'Are things better without Bella?' Nellie asked rather bluntly.

'Well, yes, they are. I'm sorry.'

'Don't be. I'm sure she's much better in the boarding school the head recommended. It was a bit of a shock at the time but she seems a different child now she's getting more help. She's coming home tomorrow for a few days. You'll see for yourself.'

'That's nice. She'll get to see the celebrations.'

'Come and choose some jewels. They're in the safe in my room.'

Paula followed her mother-in-law upstairs and into her room. Nothing much had changed since she had shared it with her husband. In fact, possibly nothing much had changed since Nellie's own mother-in-law had used it. She looked round with interest, as she had rarely been in there.

'I'll just open it and you can look at

some of the things. There's jewels in here I've never even worn. Would I be terrible if I were to sell some of them?'

'Of course not. Not if you don't wear them. It seems pointless keeping things you don't even like very much.'

Nellie took out a heap of boxes and laid them on the bed. She opened them to reveal a dazzling display of precious items: necklaces, rings, bracelets and brooches, all heaped together. There were even three tiaras, rather old-fashioned-looking but with lovely diamonds making them flash in the dim light.

'Wow,' Paula breathed. 'Have you worn them? The tiaras, I mean?'

'I used to wear them when we had rather ostentatious dinner parties. Oh look — that pendant was the one that one of the cleaners pawned. Goodness me, that was so long ago.'

'It's lovely. They all are. But I'm not sure they are all exactly fashionable today. Not unless we were invited to the palace, that is.'

Nellie was lost for a while as she

remembered times past. Then she spoke again. 'I'd like you to have something. Wait, I know the very thing.' She dived back into the safe and produced another box. 'Here. You'll like this, I'm sure.'

Paula opened the case. Inside lay a necklace of diamonds and emeralds, set alternately.

'Oh, it's beautiful. But I can't take this. It must be worth a fortune.'

'I'd like you to have it. James bought it for me a long time ago, when he'd done a massive deal with someone or other. Go on, you take it. You've got a green dress you can wear it with.'

'It's so beautiful. But can I leave it in the safe? I haven't really got anywhere to keep it. Goodness me, fancy me owning diamonds. Are you really sure?'

'I'd be delighted for you to have it. I doubt I'll ever wear it again anyway. Look at this lot. How on earth can I ever wear all of them again? Look, these were Mrs Cobridge's.' She showed her some very old-fashioned-looking pieces

— brooches that hadn't been worn for well over thirty years and some rather heavy necklaces. 'Do you think I might get something for them?'

'I would have thought so. Even if they were broken up for the stones, they must be worth quite a sum.'

'Hmm. Perhaps I'll get a jeweller to come and value them. Think of that crown the queen is going to wear. What on earth must those jewels be worth?'

'Priceless. I doubt anyone in the world has enough money to buy them. If they were ever for sale of course. I've never seen the Crown Jewels, have you?'

'I haven't. We should take a trip to London when all the fuss is over. Go and look at them. I think they're kept in the Tower, aren't they? Let's arrange a weekend. We'll stay in a large hotel and do all the tripper sorts of things.'

'It sounds lovely. I'm sure William would enjoy it.'

'We'll wait till the holidays and then we can take Bella too.' Paula smiled, knowing a trip to London with Bella could be quite a problem. Still, if it was what Nellie wanted, she knew they'd enjoy it . . . somehow.

*　*　*

They all watched the coronation ceremony in absolute fascination. The glittering golden coach carrying the young queen rolled through the streets of London, cheered on by many thousands of people.

'I wouldn't like to have been sitting out on those streets for days, would you, Wyn?' Paula's mother said.

'Certainly not. Wouldn't have done either of us much good, would it, dear?'

'I don't think I'd have liked to go to London at all, not at this time,' added Paula. 'It all seems much too busy for my liking. Oh look, isn't that the Archbishop of Canterbury? Goodness, what a responsibility.'

'I expect it's his big moment in life. There can't be so many people who actually crown the monarch. I wonder how long she'll reign?'

'She's very young. Probably quite a long time. Women do seem stronger than men in some ways. Look at Queen Victoria.'

'Hush now. Let's listen to this bit.'

Downstairs the family were all watching, intent on the television. The children were starting to get bored and asking how much longer it was going on for. Nellie produced some books with cut-outs in them. 'Look, you can make your own coaches, just like the one the queen is riding in.'

'Thanks, Nellie. They're lovely.' Soon they were all occupied with making their coaches, and the smallest one asking for help. His mother helped him, still watching intently.

They all watched as the queen was crowned. Tears were wiped surreptitiously away. She came out of the abbey to masses of cheers. It began to rain quite hard but nobody minded. The queen and her handsome husband got into the golden coach and began the procession back to the palace.

'I don't know how on earth she can bear the weight of that crown on her head.' Nellie was marvelling at her majesty's poise. 'Oh, and look at her! She doesn't mind the rain, does she?' Queen Sa-lote Tupou III was waving happily at everyone from her open coach.

At last it was all over. A huge sense of anticlimax invaded them all. William was thinking about the mass of plates he'd seen through and all the thousands of mugs. And now, it was all over. Anything that was left would be sold off at half price, he shouldn't wonder. Paula was thinking about the children's excitement and how they'd all settle down again. Her mother and aunt were simply re-living the whole event, remembering little things each of them would treasure to the end of their lives.

'Shall we go down for tea now?' William asked.

'I should think so,' Paula replied. 'The others will all be ready, won't they? I must admit, I'm jolly hungry.

The sandwiches were fine but they leave quite a gap.'

'I don't know where you put it all and still stay so slim,' Wyn remarked.

'An inherited talent,' laughed Paula.

They all went down together and greeted the rest of the family, exchanging views on the events of the day.

'Tea won't be long,' Nellie said. 'Cook prepared it all before the service so she could watch with the rest of us. Does anyone want a drink? William, will you see to everyone?'

'Of course, Mother. Joe, what do you want?'

'I'll have a beer if you've got some. Ta.'

William got drinks for everyone, and together they all raised their glasses to the health of the new queen. The little ones had orange juice and thought it was most exciting to clink their glasses together. Once more, Cook had excelled herself with the food she had laid on. She had made several coronation specials she had read about in magazines.

Coronation chicken was a particular favourite and everyone agreed the chicken in mayonnaise with curry powder was a great success. She and Sarah joined the family in their celebrations and though they were slightly embarrassed, managed to eat a sizeable tea. In the centre of the table was a magnificent cake. Cook had really gone to town and decorated in red and blue on white icing. There was a tiny model of the coach on top. Everyone agreed it was a pity to cut it, but nobody refused a hefty slice.

The family went back into the drawing room and sat drinking and talking for quite some time. Even Bella was well behaved, and she seemed to have settled well into her new school. At last Jenny suggested it was time they were going home. The party then broke up and everyone left.

'It's time you were going to bed now, Bella,' said Nellie. 'You've had a nice long time up.'

'Oh, why do you have to spoil my day?' she grumbled. 'The little ones won't be going to bed for ages yet.'

'You can see everyone off and then it's up to bed for you. I'll come and see you in bed.'

'Will you tell me a story?'

'Of course. Now, has everyone got everything they came with?'

'Thanks very much, Nellie. Lovely day. And I love your new tea set. Those plates with coronation badges on them are lovely.'

'Thanks, Jenny. I'm going to give you all a plate as a commemoration but at the moment, they're all dirty.'

They laughed as they set off home in their cars. William ran Paula's mother and aunt back to their home and the two women who were left went back inside.

'It's been quite a day,' said Nellie. 'I wonder what the queen's doing now? I expect she's having a bit of a rest before they start on the next lot of celebrations.'

'Probably having a large gin and tonic and sitting with her feet up.'

'Oh do you think so?'

'I read somewhere that's her favourite tipple.'

'No, not a young girl like that. I expect they're having some huge banquet. I wonder if they're using any of our plates?'

'I bet they've got a gold set of everything. Golden goblets for the wine and golden plates for everyone.'

'Go on with you. I bet they eat off china like the rest of us.' They both laughed. 'Well, I'd better see Bella off to bed now. Do stay down with me, won't you? I don't feel like being on my own. Not this evening.'

'Very well. I'll wait till William's back and we'll sit in the drawing room with you. I expect there'll be more things on television.' She went and sat down. She put the television on again and watched the news. When William came back, she was able to tell him about the conquest of Everest.

'I hadn't heard about it till now,' he said.

'What a day. I wonder when they climbed it? Must have been at least a day or two ago. Must have kept it quiet till today so they could announce it all at the same time.' Nellie came back into the room. 'Mother, have you heard the latest news? They've conquered Everest. Edmund Hillary and someone called Tenzing Norgay. Amazing, isn't it?'

'It's certainly been quite a day. I've got a bottle of champagne ready for us to share. Will you do the honours, William?'

'Lovely. Course I will.' He opened it and his mother brought him the glasses to pour it out.

'Here's to the royal family. Long may she reign,' said Nellie.

'The royal family,' the others joined in the toast.

'And to the men who conquered Everest,' added William.

'To the men who conquered Everest,' the others echoed.

'What a day to remember,' Paula said. 'I feel quite teary now. It's all over.

Everything we've been leading up to for so long, and now it's over.'

'We've got the rest of our lives to look forward to,' said William.

'Oh I know all that. Somehow, though, I haven't really looked beyond today.'

'I know what you mean,' said Nellie. 'I'm rather glad I gave the factory workers another day off. I shall take Bella back to her school tomorrow and make sure she's settling in properly. Come on now, drink up. We must finish off the bottle.'

As they went to bed, they thought about the thousands of people who were making their way back home from London. Some of them were probably people they knew. Some of the people from the factory had been talking about making the trip.

'I do feel slightly squiffy,' Paula announced as they got into bed. 'I don't think I should have drunk quite so much.'

'Never mind. You'll soon sleep it off.'

The next morning however, when Paula got up, she felt very sick. She rushed along to the toilet and was actually sick.

'Are you all right, love?' asked William, rather concerned.

'Not really. I feel awful. I think I'd better go back to bed.'

'You do that. I'll bring you some tea, shall I?'

'Just water please.' She sat back on the edge of the bed and wondered if she was actually going to make it to lie down.

'You look very pale. Shall I call the doctor?'

'Oh goodness no. I'll be all right in a while. Must have eaten something that disagreed with me.'

'Maybe. I'll call Mother. She'll know what to do.'

'Please don't. I don't want any fuss. Just leave me alone and get yourself some breakfast. I'll be better soon.'

Doubtfully, he went to the kitchen and made some tea. He remembered her water and took it in to her. She was lying down with her eyes closed so he left it near to her and went back and made some toast. He went downstairs to collect the papers and then sat looking at endless pictures of the previous day's events. He felt restless, wondering what to do on his own. He went back to look at Paula. She was sitting up looking much better.

'Sorry about that,' she said. 'I don't know what it was but I'm feeling better now. I think I'll get up soon.'

'Are you sure? Stay in bed for the morning. Do you want anything?'

'I wouldn't say no to some toast, actually.'

'I'll go and make it. What do you want on it?'

'Marmite.'

'But you hate marmite.'

'Do I? I really fancy some please. If I don't like it, you can have it.' Shaking his head, he left her and went to make some toast. He went back into the bedroom with a plate of marmite on toast and the papers.

'There's a supplement with pictures from yesterday. I was thinking we might keep it.'

'Along with everyone else in the country. Still, it's a nice idea. Is your mother around yet?'

'I heard her bumping round. Or maybe it was Bella doing the bumping.'

'She does seem a lot better, don't you think?'

'Oh yes. Heaps. I suppose it's having the right situation around her and people who actually know what to do with her. Much better than her sitting in the kitchen making a nuisance of herself with Cook.'

'This toast is scrumptious. Thank you, darling.'

'I'll never understand you. For someone who hates marmite, you've made short work of that lot.'

'Perhaps it's the start of my new passion.' He looked at her fondly, still shaking his head.

12

When the sickness happened again the next day, Paula became suspicious. She looked at her diary and discovered that she was also late. She sat down heavily. She must be pregnant, she realised. How on earth would she cope with having a baby? Thinking about it, she was quite old enough, older than many people, and she was actually rather excited. She made an appointment to see the doctor. A week later, she knew for sure.

'I've got something to tell you, William,' she announced after supper. 'I'm going to have a baby.'

'Oh Paula, that's terrific. I couldn't be happier. You must resign from your position at school. Another few weeks and you'll be breaking up for the summer. They won't miss you for the rest of term.'

'Don't be silly. Why on earth would I give up teaching? Not yet, anyway.'

'But you can't go on. I insist you give up right away.'

'No. I'll think about giving up at the end of term but I'm not stopping before then. Heavens, your ladies go on for months before they give up work.'

'They need the money. One thing you don't need is extra money.'

'But what will I do all day? I'll go crazy with nothing to do.'

'I was thinking. We really should look for a place of our own. It's silly us staying in this bit of the house. I know it's lovely. Mother did it all beautifully but it's going to be too small with a baby.'

'You are pleased, aren't you?'

'Course I am. I'm delighted. Clever girl. But you need to be very careful. Sit with your feet up and everything.'

'Oh please, don't make such a fuss. I'm not ill. I'm going to sail through my pregnancy like clockwork. And don't tell anyone yet. I only just know and it's much too soon.'

'Why? What's wrong?'

'Oh William, William. Nothing's wrong. I just want to keep it between us for a while. When I'm nearly three months, then will be soon enough to tell everyone.'

'So how long is it?'

'About seven weeks. Or thereabouts.'

'But that's ages till we can tell everyone.'

'So be it. The mother-to-be has spoken.'

'Well, it's certainly something to be excited about. And to think, this time last week you were moaning about anticlimax when the coronation was all over.'

There came a knock at their door.

'Nellie. Come in.'

'I've just had a telephone call from the place where Bella is. She's gone missing.'

'What?' William came to the door.

'Yes, she went off to play after supper and now they can't find her. They think she may be trying to get home. Some squabble or other with another child.'

'Oh no. Have they looked everywhere?'

'They say so. They've got people out looking for her.'

'But surely she'll never make it all the way home? It's too far.'

'I'm going to drive over there now. I wondered if you'd come with me?'

'Of course we will,' said Paula. 'I'll get my coat.'

'No, dear. You stay here. I'll drive us,' William insisted.

'Don't be silly. I'm coming too. I'd be left here wondering and it would drive me mad.'

'But should you be going out?'

'Why on earth shouldn't she?' Nellie asked, looking even more confused.

'Of course there's no reason for me to me left behind. Now, can we stop arguing and get on our way?'

It was almost dark when they set off. They drove slowly through the lanes, all of them looking for the little girl, even though they were too far away from the centre for her to have reached that point.

'We're assuming she'd have walked along the road,' said Nellie. 'S'posin' she went over the fields?'

'Would she have done that? I'm sure she'd come along the road,' Paula said.

'I don't know. I never know what she'll do next. And just when we thought as she were doin' okay.' Nellie was reverting to her natural accent in her distress. 'I should never have let her go there.'

'Of course you should. You weren't coping, were you? She was left to manage on her own such a lot.'

'Mebbe I took on too much when I took over at Cobridge's. I should have stayed home to look after my daughter.'

'Now Nellie, you mustn't talk like that,' Paula said. 'Bella was always a difficult child. I couldn't really cope with her at school, could I? I encour- aged you to send her away. It's just as much my fault as yours.'

William looked at his wife, appreciating how much that statement had cost her to say. It was an indictment of her professionalism in a way. He spoke again. 'I expect it was a silly argument with someone. You know what Bella's like. She probably simply ran out of the building and is hiding somewhere. Have they looked under her bed? She's probably hiding there. Remember the tea party, when she stayed under her bed the whole afternoon?'

'Do I?' remarked Nellie. 'I'm sure they'll have looked there. They said they'd looked all round the building.'

'Well, we're nearly there. It's round the next corner, isn't it?'

'I think so, yes. There's the gates into the drive.'

'Left open, I see.'

'They can't lock them cos of all the people coming and going. Drive up to the doors. Let's see what's going off.' Nellie jumped out almost before William had stopped the car. She banged on the door, obviously very upset. It was opened by a quiet-looking man. 'Have you found her?' she demanded.

'I'm afraid not. We have a team of staff out looking for her. Come on in; I'll explain it all to you. Oh, and this is your son and daughter-in-law? Oh yes, we met during the assessment, didn't we?'

'Hallo, Mr Downs. Yes, indeed, we've met.' Paula assumed a more professional air as she spoke to him. 'Can you tell us exactly what happened?'

'Indeed yes. Come into my office. I'll try to explain.' They followed him in and sat in a circle. 'Bella is a strong character, as you know. After they had eaten supper, she seemed to have an argument with the boy she was next to. She hit him across the cheek, reducing him to tears. Then she got up and ran out of the room. The staff on duty were concerned with the injured child, who was screaming and upsetting the other children. We didn't realise she was missing for a while, I'm afraid. We assumed she'd gone up to her room.

Once the child was pacified, my staff went to look for her.'

'But surely the door was kept locked,' Nellie said.

'Indeed yes. We suspect she climbed out of a window. In the kitchen.' He raised his eyes towards heaven. 'She often went there. Trying to get extra cakes or something.'

'She does that at home. I'm surprised you let her do it here,' Nellie remarked.

'We try not to put too many restrictions on our charges. It can inhibit their progress.'

'Well, it didn't work in Bella's case, did it?' Nellie snapped. 'I really find it hard to believe a little girl can get out so easily. You really need to tighten up on your security.'

'I can assure you we will. I hate having too many locks on doors and too many rules and regulations. As I said, we like our pupils to learn what is the right thing to do.'

'It's all very well arguing the toss, but shouldn't we be out there looking?'

William suggested. 'We're not doing any good sitting here like this.'

'I'm not sure where else to look to be honest. We thought she might have set out towards home but as you came that way, we assume you didn't see her.' Mr Downs looked somewhat crestfallen.

'You have thoroughly searched the building?'

'Oh yes, of course.'

'Even looked under her bed?'

'I beg your pardon?'

'Well, she's spent time hidden under her bed at home,' Nellie told him.

'She couldn't really hide under there. It's a high bed, off the ground.'

'Can I look?' asked Nellie.

'You can look. But she isn't there. And nor is she in the wardrobe,' he added.

They all trooped upstairs to Bella's room. It was a small, pleasant room with nice pictures on the walls. It was clearly empty.

'Bathrooms?' Nellie asked.

'This way,' said Mr Downs, knowing

they had all been searched already.

'And you've looked in the other rooms?'

'Of course. Every one.'

'Well then, we make a start on the outside.' Nellie was clearly not leaving anywhere without her personal, proper search.

'I can assure you, my staff have all looked very carefully round the buildings. Bella is indeed a law unto herself.'

They all trooped round outside in the now-darkening evening. William kept asking Paula if she was all right. Nellie listened and wondered why he was so concerned. But her mind was on finding her daughter. It reached almost ten o'clock.

'We're never going to find her, are we?' Nellie moaned.

'It's looking less likely,' said Mr Downs miserably. 'I'm going to call the police now. I'm sure she isn't on the premises. Why don't you all go home now and leave me to sort out the police?'

'I think it may be best, Mother.

Don't you think so, Paula?'

'I do really. We can look along the road as we drive back. The police will conduct a thorough search, I'm sure.' Though she was feeling very weary, she doubted that she would actually sleep, not with Bella missing out in the wilds on her own.

'I'll phone you as soon as we hear anything,' promised Mr Downs.

Nellie seemed numb with shock. Automatically, she got into the car and allowed herself to be driven home. They drove slowly to begin with, all looking out for a small child wandering along the road. They sped up the nearer home they got; and once there, Nellie rushed inside to see if anyone had heard anything. Cook greeted her, looking very anxious.

'We ain't not 'eard owt,' she said.

'There's no sign of her round the school. I think when she's been found, I'll have her home again. I can't be doin' with all this.'

'I'm sure she'll be fine, Mother,' said

William. 'You know what she's like. She'll turn up with a smile on her face, wondering why anyone missed her at all.'

'I just hope you're right. Silly little madam. I'll give her such a spanking for worrying us like this.'

'You go up and go to bed, Paula. You've got school tomorrow as usual, and you need some sleep.'

'Sleep? Don't be ridiculous. I'll never manage to sleep.'

'You need to look after yourself.'

'Is there something you're not telling me?' asked Nellie. 'Some good news?'

'Well yes. Paula's pregnant. We only found out today.'

'Congratulations, dear. I hope you make a better job of it than I did.'

'You did a marvellous job.'

'Oh yes? One turned into a snob and the other's bonkers.'

'Stop it, Mother. I'm not a snob and Bella certainly isn't bonkers, as you put it. Go and sit down and Cook'll make you a hot drink.'

'Course I will. What do you fancy? Cocoa? Tea or coffee?'

'I'd love some cocoa. Comfort sort of thing.'

'What about the rest on ya?'

'Yes please,' replied Paula.

'Might as well join in with the others,' William told her. She bustled off and they all sat down in the hall to be near the telephone, in case it should ring. Cook came back with a jug of cocoa. It was an anxious group, all of them feeling worried and also tired. Paula could hardly stop yawning.

'Please go up to bed, love,' William said. 'You'll be fit for nothing tomorrow.'

'I can't leave you all now.'

'You go up,' Nellie said. 'William'll come and tell you if there's any news, won't you, love?'

'Course I will. Go on. Upstairs with you.'

'Very well then. Let me know as soon as you hear anything. Night, Nellie. And don't worry too much. Knowing

Bella, she'll be hiding somewhere, laughing at the sight of everyone hunting for her.' She went up to the apartment and realised she hadn't even washed up their supper things. She dumped them in the sink and ran water over them. Tomorrow would be soon enough. She lay on top of their bed, fully clothed in case she needed to get up again quickly. She didn't expect to sleep at all but soon she was fast asleep.

Nellie and William sat in the drawing room, the door propped open to hear the phone. They sat in the big chairs and both of them fell into an exhausted, light doze.

13

It was six o'clock before the phone finally rang. Nellie leapt up to answer it. 'Hallo?' she said.

'It's Mr Downs here.'

'Yes? Have you found her?'

'I'm afraid not. I'm just calling to keep in touch as I agreed.'

'Oh dear, no. I'll come over again.'

'There's no need. The police are now all out looking. I'm sure we'll find her soon.'

'I should bloody well hope so. I'll sue you if you don't.' In a temper brought on by her anxiety, she banged the phone down.

'I take it there's no news.' William had listened to one side of the call.

'Nothing at all. I'm going over there again. I might be able to help with the search somehow. Do you think you could go into the factory? I have various meetings arranged. You can either take them yourself or cancel them. Look in my diary. They're all listed there. My secretary keeps it up-to-date for me.'

'Of course I will. But wouldn't you rather I came with you?'

'No. You go and sort out the factory. Then at least I'll know it's happening as it should. Damn Bella. She always causes as much trouble as she possibly can, doesn't she?'

'I'll go up and see how Paula is and change. I'll have a quick bath as well. I feel very grubby.'

'I'll go and change as well. Do you want me to ask Cook to get some breakfast for you?'

'It's okay. I'll get something with Paula.'

He went upstairs and found Paula fast asleep on top of the bed. He leaned over her to kiss her.

'Any news?' she asked.

'Nothing. I'm going to have a quick bath and change, and then I'm going to the factory to hold Mother's various meetings. She's going back to the school, threatening them with all sorts. How are you?'

'Tired. And I feel . . . sick.' She leapt up and ran to the bathroom. William felt at a loss to know what to do. Someone should be able to do something for the poor woman. It may be nature, but it was terrible to have to watch and be able to do nothing. She came back looking awful.

'Sit down for a minute. Till you're feeling a bit better,' he said feebly.

'I'll have to stay still for a while. You go and get on.'

'I'll make some toast in a minute. It might help you to have something inside you.'

'To throw up again? Thanks.'

He went and got himself ready for work. A clean shirt and change of clothes made all the difference. He made toast for them both and Paula managed to eat a little.

'Will you be all right going to school? I could drive you there if you like.'

'I'll be fine. A walk will do me good. Besides, I can see you're ready to go now. I need to do a few things before I go. Go on. Go and be the boss.' He smiled at her words and set out, checking to see where his mother was before he left the house. She had already gone.

By the end of the morning, William felt totally exhausted. He knew it was partly the fact that he hadn't slept properly, but also it was the pace at which his mother worked. He'd had four different meetings, all of which had needed decisions making, and he prayed he'd given them the answers as his mother would have done. The various managers had gone looking happy, so he assumed he'd given the right answers. He picked up the phone to ring Bella's school.

'Haven't you found my sister yet?' he asked incredulously. 'I really don't understand. I bet my mother's furious.'

'I'm sorry, Mr Cobridge. I don't know what else I can say. Mr Downs has been up all night and even now, he is out looking.' The secretary, or whatever she was, sounded sincere enough but very defensive of her boss.

'Can I speak to my mother please? Get her to call me if she isn't there.'

'I'll pass on your message. Can you give me your number?'

'She knows where I am.' He slammed the phone down, wondering what he should do. Should he go and join the search? It seemed a bit pointless, but he wanted to do something. His phone rang, and again he was in the thick of being in charge of the factory.

* * *

Nellie was almost dropping with fatigue. She had insisted on walking round with everyone, beating under bushes and poking sticks into clumps of longer growing grass. It seemed that loads of people from the village had come to join the hunt. They had been organised into groups, each given an area to search thoroughly.

'We're looking for a body, aren't we?' she said tearfully to Mr Downs. 'You don't believe she's even still alive. But she is. I'd know if she wasn't.'

'I think you should come back and eat something. Come on now. There are plenty of people searching. You won't really be missed here.'

'I'd love a cup of tea,' she admitted.

'Come on then. Back to the school.'

Wearily, they walked back to the school building and went inside. Nellie felt grubby and tired beyond all reason. She slumped down in the hallway and sat staring into space. Mr Downs went off to organise some tea and something for them both to eat.

'Come into my office. It will be more peaceful in there. They'll tell us as soon as there's any news.'

'Thank you. You're very kind.' He looked as exhausted as she did. Someone from the kitchen came in with a plate of sandwiches and tea. She poured them each a cup and left them.

Nellie tried to eat but the bread

tasted like cardboard. She drank the tea, however, and felt marginally better.

'What on earth do we do if we can't find her?' asked the anxious mother.

'We'll find her. We've never had a child go missing before. But then, we haven't had a child quite like Bella before.'

'That's no comfort to me, I'm afraid. I'd like to go and look some more.'

'Very well. Are you sure you can't eat another sandwich?'

'No thanks.'

The doorbell rang. 'I'd better see who that is. The staff left inside are all busy with our other clients.'

Nellie stayed in his office, waiting till he came back. He burst into the room. 'Look who's here,' he said, dragging Bella in behind him.

'Bella! Wherever have you been? You naughty girl, going off like that.' She gathered her into her arms and hugged her as she was telling her off. She looked up and saw an old lady standing in the doorway, looking somewhat scared.

'It's Mrs Bishop. She lives in a little place in the woods. She brought your daughter back.'

'Thank you, Mrs Bishop. How did you find her?'

'Beggin' your pardon, ma'am. Er came to me last night. Sat 'ersen down and then fell asleep. I arksed 'er where she'd come frae but 'er dint wake up.'

'When was this?' Nellie asked.

'Last neet. Ah didna know who 'er was, nor that folks was art lookin' for 'er.'

'Well, I think we need to thank you very much for taking care of her.'

'S'or reet. I'll be goin' now. Now 'er's back where 'er should be.'

'I'll see you to the door,' said Mr Downs. 'And my thanks are added to those of Mrs Cobridge.'

'Cobridge? Ah knows that name. Ya know Vera? 'er's ma girl.'

'Really? I didn't know that. I take it you haven't seen her for some time?'

'Nah. 'er don't want to know me. Not no more.'

'I see. I'll mention you to her when I

see her again. She's retired now of course. Now Bella, do you want something to eat? Thank you again, Mrs Bishop.' The old lady left them and Mr Downs went to see her out. He came back into the room.

'Well, thank goodness all's well that ends well,' he said. 'I'd better call the police and see if they can tell all the people searching.'

'I need to phone William too. He'll be so relieved. Have a sandwich, Bella. There are plenty there.'

'Don't want one. They're horrible.'

'They're not. They're lovely. Please yourself. Have you had anything to eat today?'

'Mrs Bishop gave me some breakfast about five minutes ago.'

It took a while to get the whole story sorted out. It seemed that Bella had indeed climbed out of the kitchen window and had run off into the woods. She had arrived at Mrs Bishop's cottage, though that was a rather grand name for the place, and she took her in. Bella had told her she was lost, and then she sat down in a chair and fell asleep. She didn't wake till this morning, when the lady had finally got out of her where she lived. It was then she brought her back to the school.

'I hope you won't hold it against us, Mrs Cobridge. I can assure you that we normally never have our clients disappearing like that.'

'I can understand. I won't be removing Bella from your care. She really has improved such a lot since she's been here. Can I see her again before I go?'

'Of course. I'll go and find her.'

She had been taken up to the bathroom and given a bath. By the time she re-appeared, she was clean and wearing a different dress. Looking as innocent as a daisy, she stood in the office and smiled at her mother.

'I'm going home now, dear,' Nellie told her. 'I want you to be good, and no more running away.' Bella smiled at her but there was a glint in her eye. 'Promise me you won't try to run off again?'

She scowled and then decided. 'All right. As long as I can come home again soon.'

'If you're good,' Nellie promised. 'Bye-bye now. Give me a hug.' She did, and then bounced away as if nothing had happened. 'I hope she doesn't give us all such a worry again.'

They said their goodbyes and wearily Nellie drove back home. *Forget about going into work*, she told herself. It was time William was really learning to take over.

When he came home that evening, he went straight in to see his mother. 'How was Bella?' he asked.

'She was fine. Absolutely fine.'

'She's still there, then?'

'Oh yes. Mr Downs persuaded me she'd be best left there.'

'Oh good. That's a huge relief. I was afraid she'd have got round you to bring her back here. She needs to stay where she is.' He paused and then spoke again. 'The meetings all went very well this morning. I think everyone is clear about what they're doing. Now if you'll excuse me, I'm going up to see Paula. Make sure she's feeling all right.'

'I saw her when she came home. She certainly looked quite well. Morning sickness never lasts forever, you know. It's distressing at the time but it's soon over. And William, well done for today. You are going to be a real asset to the company. Your father would be proud of you.'

'Thank you, Mother. That's what I needed to know. And you must let me run more of the meetings. I'm more than capable.'

'I begin to see that you are. Now go up to Paula. Give her my love.'

She sat in James's chair and thought about her future. She really believed there was a future now. With William and Paula starting their own family, she was going to be a grandma. She spoke aloud: 'So, James, you may have left me alone — but you know what? I'm going to manage things with William's help. Cobridge's has a future.'

HER HEART'S DESIRE
FROM THIS DAY ON
WHERE THE HEART IS
OUT OF THE BLUE
TOMORROW'S DREAMS
DARE TO LOVE
WHERE LOVE BELONGS
TO LOVE AGAIN
DESTINY CALLING
THE SURGEON'S MISTAKE
GETTING A LIFE